Photo credit: Tina FiveAsh

Sarah Brill grew up in Perth and began writing at the age of 15. She initially focused on playwrighting but also wrote for film and radio. Her play *Who the Fuck is Erica Price* was first performed in 1996 and is still occasionally performed today. Her first novel, *Glory*, which dealt with anorexia, was published by Spinifex Press in 2002. After the birth of her children Sarah became interested in sustainability and permaculture. In 2017 she completed a Masters of Sustainable Built Environment and currently works for a local government council in resource recovery. Sarah lives in Sydney with her partner and three sons. *Symphony for the Man* is her second novel.

Other books by Sarah Brill

Glory (2002)

SYMPHONY FOR THE MAN

Sarah Brill

First published by Spinifex Press, 2020

Reprinted 2020

Spinifex Press Pty Ltd
PO Box 5270, North Geelong, VIC 3215, Australia
PO Box 105, Mission Beach, QLD 4852, Australia

women@spinifexpress.com.au
www.spinifexpress.com.au

Copyright © Sarah Brill, 2020

The moral right of the author has been asserted.

All rights reserved. Without limiting the rights under copyright
reserved above, no part of this publication may be reproduced,
stored in or introduced into a retrieval system, or transmitted,
in any form or by any means (electronic, mechanical, photocopying,
recording or otherwise) without prior written permission of both
the copyright owner and the above publisher of the book.

Copying for educational purposes
Information in this book may be reproduced in whole or part for
study or training purposes, subject to acknowledgement of the source
and providing no commercial usage or sale of material occurs.
Where copies of part or whole of the book are made under part VB
of the Copyright Act, the law requires that prescribed procedures
be followed. For information contact the Copyright Agency Limited.

Edited by Pauline Hopkins, Renate Klein and Susan Hawthorne
Cover design by Deb Snibson, MAPG
Typesetting by Helen Christie, Blue Wren Books
Typeset in Berling
Printed by McPherson's Printing Group

 A catalogue record for this book is available from the National Library of Australia

ISBN: 9781925950069 (paperback)
ISBN: 9781925950076 (ebook)

*This book is for those of us who
dream big while living on government subsidies
that are too small.*

It's winter, 1999, the first time I see him from the bus. He looks lost. Lonely. Cold. I think about what I could do for him. How I could help. I think about it from Bondi to Circular Quay. I think about sitting next to him and talking. I think about giving him all the money I have. I think about taking him home and putting him in a bath and making him soup from scratch. I think of all these things and more and none of them seem right. So I do nothing. But I think about it. I think about what he needs and what I could give him. I decide to write a symphony. A symphony for the man I saw from the bus.

FIRST

Harry has always liked seagulls. He likes the whiteness of their feathers and the way they always look so neat and clean even though they live off scraps. He likes the way they move on land. How they use their wings to cover ground faster if there's food around. He likes watching them as they stand in groups. At first he can't tell one from the other, but the longer he watches the more he sees. He sees they are individuals, marked by a fluffed out feather here, a leg missing there.

Harry likes seagulls in the afternoon, when it's warm and there's a gentle breeze. He likes to sit in the park next to the beach and watch them beg for food, pick through the bins, argue among themselves. He hates them in the morning when he wakes to find them searching through his pockets, shitting on his clothes, crying in his ear.

And that's how he wakes up this morning. A bloody seagull sitting on his chest, pecking at him, shitting on him. It's not a good way to wake up, and Harry doesn't much like waking up anyway. He lets out a bit of a yell that scares the bird off and then he lies back down to listen to the noise of the traffic and think about the day ahead.

He lies on his bench as long as he can. He knows it will be cold getting up and he doesn't feel ready to face it. He thinks about Queensland and whether he could ever move there. He thinks about whether it really is warm all the time or whether those buggers who have been just make that shit up. He thinks about Tony who's been gone a few days now. Maybe he's there. Maybe Harry should go too. But Harry is like the seagulls. The ones that stay at the beach all year round. They stay because it's their home. Because they know where things are and it doesn't really matter that it's cold or wet. Not as much as it matters about knowing where things are.

Then Harry reads the graffiti the way he's done a thousand times before and he wonders how Nik and Rachel are and if they really do still love each other. He reads the bit he tried to scrub off one day with a bit of water and an old shirt. The bit that says "this way out" and has an arrow under it pointing to the road. He doesn't think about who might have written it. One day it wasn't there, the next day it was. He doesn't think about it any more.

Harry sticks his hands out from under his blanket to test the temperature of the air. Then he gets up in one quick motion. Like ripping off a bandaid. Or at least that's what he tells himself. If you saw him you wouldn't think it was one quick motion. It looks like a slow, hard climb. Stiff joints, painful back, aching legs. But to Harry it's one quick motion, like ripping off a bandaid. Then he's up, folding his blanket nice and neat, brushing his teeth. Harry doesn't have toothpaste but he does have a toothbrush so every morning after Harry rips off the bandaid, he brushes his teeth.

He hears her before he sees her. That gentle squeak of the pram wheels. That clip of her heels against the concrete. He panics. He's thinking, "Shit, it's Jules," and he wishes it was her that woke him up instead of the bloody seagull. It's a nice thing to wake up to, that gentle squeak and small clip. He wishes he'd stayed where he was, wishes he'd waited till she'd passed before he ripped off the bandaid. That way he could really take her in, see what she's wearing and how the kid is looking. That's how he learnt her entire wardrobe. Learnt to know how she was feeling depending on what she was wearing. That's how he watched her kid change from a squirming pink thing to the fat little hairy, toothy bugger he is now.

But today Jules is going to catch him with his shirt hanging out and his toothbrush in his mouth. Her kid will probably burst into tears at the sight of him. And even though he's desperate to see what she's wearing, desperate to know how she's feeling today, he can't do it. So he stands in the corner of the bus shelter, his face to the wall, toothbrush still in his mouth. He listens as the pram gets closer and he feels like a naughty child. A schoolboy sent to the corner for swearing. He panics, sweats, tries not to shake and hopes he will just disappear into the paintwork.

The squeak of the pram gets closer. The gentle clip of her heels gets louder until she's right there, right behind him. Harry squeezes his eyes closed tight and tries to make himself smaller. Then he hears the kid carrying on in his pram. They're nearly past the bus stop but the kid has started crying and the squeak and the clip stops and her voice rings out. "What's the matter Kieran?" Her voice is soft and kind. "You hungry darling?"

Harry's legs start to shake wildly as he imagines her sitting down right there and then in his shelter so she can feed the kid. Harry thinks about running. About turning around and running as fast as he can away from that bus shelter but, before he gets the nerve to move, the squeaking starts up again. That gentle clip of her heels moves away and Harry is free. Now he can sit. Rest his shaking legs.

He doesn't though. He stands there like the idiot he feels he is until he can hear nothing but the traffic. And then he stands a bit longer. Just to be sure. He can't get the idea out of his head that it's some kind of trick. That he's going to turn around and she'll still be there.

When Harry can no longer stand, he turns around and sees that she really is gone. Then he sits down. He takes the toothbrush out of his mouth and he waits for the shaking in his legs to stop.

And that's it. That's the best part of Harry's day just passed. And he spent it scared and shaking and staring at the corner of his bus shelter. But at least, for those long few minutes, he could pretend that Jules was passing by with her baby. He will spend the rest of the day looking for the real Jules. Not actively searching, not any more. But looking. Looking at the women who go by, at the cars and buses. Wondering, is that the bus that's holding Jules?

In the early days Harry would sit outside the old apartment block. He'd sit there for hours. Those were the days when he'd smoke and drink. Smoke and drink and sit, hour after hour. He didn't want to speak to Jules, didn't want to bother her, just wanted to see her, wanted to know she was all right. He didn't particularly care whether she had a baby with her or not. The baby wasn't the thing he thought about. He just wanted to know she was all right.

She walks off the bus that day with her thoughts clouded by the sight of the man in the bus shelter and by the sky. People scurry to get out of the weather but she is not in a hurry as she moves through the crowds, past the food shops under the station, towards the clean, white sails of the Opera House.

She barely feels the rain as it hits her face and body. She doesn't feel the wind and the cold. She sees only the Opera House, the harbour beside it. It takes the clouds away, makes the wind warm. It lets her know that everything is going to be okay.

The Quay has been there for her since she first arrived in Sydney. In those early days she would catch the train from the west. She'd get on the city circle, just for the heady rush of the train bursting out into sunlight, into the Quay. She didn't notice the ugly train station, the towering office buildings behind. She saw only the Opera House, the Bridge, the ferries moving slowly in and out. When everything became hard, dark and cold, when she felt too lonely, the Quay kept her here. It made her want to stay.

She has never been good at staying. Her parents can't be blamed. They moved her once when she was a little girl. Just once. After that she grew up in the same house and went to the same school. It is not her body that got used to movement – it is her mind that is never able to be still. Her mind that has never found one thing, that one thing she is always searching for, that one thing to keep her still.

But now she has the Quay. It absorbs her. It holds her in this city while she searches for her thing. Even with the changes taking place all over the city, as it prepares for the coming Olympics, the Quay is still the Quay to her. Today she stays all morning. Sometimes walking, sometimes standing. It's too wet to sit. Sometimes she shelters but often she stands in the dripping rain. She enjoys the feeling of the rain on her face. She doesn't mind the cold because she knows at the end of it there will be a warm shower, dry clothes. Hot food.

In front of her she sees the ferries come and go. She watches other boat traffic and marvels at how they manage to avoid each other. If she squints she can make out the figures of the brave or unlucky people who have chosen this day to climb the Bridge.

She's wanted to do that since it first opened. To see the Quay from the uppermost reaches of the Bridge. But climbing the Bridge is way out of her budget. And sticking to her budget is how she survives. How she gets to stay.

When she first moved to this city she lived in the west where the housing was cheaper and the trains were close. She shared a house, tried to make friends. Followed where those friends led, looking all the time for something to cling to.

There were rock bands and student films. Café work and shopkeeping. There were brief forays into alternative political parties and information nights at the universities although she never quite made the step of enrolling. Now she regrets not studying, the way she regrets most of her past decisions.

The friends drifted away so quickly she wondered whether they were ever really there. She considered moving back home. The thought seemed like an easy way out but no real solution. And anyway the Quay already had its hold on her. Attaching her to a city too expensive for her to survive in, too big for her to truly understand. But holding her nonetheless when she had nothing else to hold onto.

So she moved to the east where she could just about afford a tiny room near the sea. It was rough and dirty. But she has her own bathroom and a tiny kitchenette. She made herself a new home in this tiny room. And it is here she has come to understand that she will never go back to where she grew up.

Back on the Quay the rain has soaked her clothes and her hair. She starts to feel the chill of the wind as she makes her way back to the bus. She notices the stares, the way people avoid sitting near her. She feels the cold of the rain on her skin and she concentrates on what it will be like when she gets home. She imagines the warmth of the shower and the softness of the clothes she will put on. These thoughts get her through the bus ride. They do not stop her lips turning blue or her hands shaking but they get her through.

When she opens the door to her apartment she is grateful for its size. For how easy the small space is to warm. She turns on the electric heater as she strips the wet clothes from her body.

The bathroom is tiny of course. She has to squeeze past the toilet to look at herself in the mirror above the sink. She stares at herself, like she does every day, unconsciously seeking beauty and finding it in part, if only in the familiarity of her face. She finds faults too, flaws in her features, more than she finds beauty. She tries not to look too long.

The shower takes a moment to heat up but when it does, the water is so hot she breathes in sharply as it hits her skin. She adds a little cold water and closes her eyes. The cold of the rain and wind are washed away from her skin and she is left pink, even a little sweaty.

Today she does not notice the mould growing between the tiles around the shower edge and on the bottom of the shower curtain. When she first moved in she scrubbed at it all the time. She was determined it could be removed. Now she lets it be. It's only on bad days that it bothers her.

Comfortable in tracksuit bottoms and a large wool jumper she found in a local charity shop, she makes herself a piece of toast with a scrape of butter. According to her budget the butter needs to last another two weeks and it is already low. The plate is chipped but one she loves. Another charity shop discovery. She's not been able to find a second like it. She's found similar but never one with this exact colouring and pattern of flowers and leaves twisting around the edge.

She stands on her balcony, plate and toast in hand, to watch the rain hit the ocean. Actually the balcony is more of an outdoor shelf. To sit she has to be cross-legged with her knees against the railing. She has come to find this position quite comfortable but only on warm days and only if she doesn't want to see the ocean.

It's time to think about the homeless man. His image has been with her the whole day. But now it's time to think properly about him. This man she saw from the bus and her decision to write a symphony for him.

It seems right to her that the homeless man needs a symphony. It seems obvious that she must be the one to write it. It's the first step she needs to decide now. Sometimes the first step is the hardest. The most important. It is the first step that will make or break a project.

She has taken a lot of wrong first steps. That's why things haven't quite worked out before now. She doesn't want to think about the awkward months she spent working on student films, convinced this would be her career for life, while her heart pumped wildly with fear anytime someone asked her to do anything because she had no idea what to actually do. She doesn't want to think about how she woke with dread at the thought of just getting herself to the set. She doesn't want think about the nights she spent awake, crunching numbers in her head, in the hope of starting a food business. About the lease she almost signed. All of these times, she thinks, she rushed, she didn't find the right first step. If this is it, if this is to be her thing, she needs to spend a bit of time thinking of what the right first step should be.

There's the local library. It has an Internet connection. Computers that the public can use. She could type in "how to write a symphony." Instructions would appear in a moment. She's sure of it. But it doesn't feel like the right step. It doesn't feel like the first step. A computer, instructions, these feel like a leap. She needs a step.

What she wants is a book. Again, there's the local library. She has a card somewhere. But that's not right either. She doesn't want a book she has to give back. She wants a book that she can keep. A book she can devour. She wants a book with no return date. A book she can drop in the bath and then dry by the heater leaving the pages waved and swollen but still readable. She wants a book she can leave her wine glass on so that a permanent red ring remains on the cover. It will be a book she can hold up on opening night or at press conferences and say, this was the start of it all. This was the book that started everything. This is the kind of book she wants. This will be the first step.

Harry still feels the shaking inside his legs as he walks down to the beach for his morning shower. Charlie's already there, Harry can smell his bags before he sees them piled up near the showers. Once Harry was around when one of them split open. He hasn't forgotten the stinking mess that poured out. Half of it unrecognisable. Couldn't touch it though, couldn't put it in the bin. That stinking mess was precious to Charlie and after all the screaming and fighting that went on that day Harry doesn't try to talk to him about it anymore.

Just near his bags, always just near his bags, is Charlie, damp from his shower. Harry doesn't say hello. He just launches into the story of his morning. It feels good to get it out. Stops most of that shake in his legs. He will let the water take away the rest. Charlie snorts at the end of the story. He says, "She probably thought you were having a wank," and Harry doesn't reply because this thought hadn't occurred to him.

Instead of answering Charlie, Harry lets himself fall into the shower. Lets the shower take away the aching, the stiffness, that tired feeling behind his eyes. He lets the shower take it all away and when he turns off the water he feels a lot better.

Charlie is gathering up his bags and preparing to leave. He throws another sentence at Harry as he walks away. "Cops got Tony." Harry hears but he doesn't listen. He's thinking about a soft fluffy towel. That would be the best thing after a shower. A soft fluffy towel. Harry thinks about towels every time he has a shower. And then he dries himself with the best thing he's got, usually his shirt, and he puts his stinking clothes back on. Every piece of clothing that goes back on his skin takes a little of the shower away, until at the end, he's fully dressed and feeling like the shower never happened. Then he thinks it's not worth it, this morning shower.

He refers to it as his morning shower though in reality it is more of a weekly event than a daily one. He makes his way down here when his body aches for the relief only a shower can bring and on those mornings he decides to forget this inevitable feeling of defeat that he's stuck with now.

It's only as he heads out to look for some breakfast that Charlie's words sink in. Tony never made it to Queensland, only made it to the lock up. Harry feels a moment's pity for Tony. No one likes to be locked up. More than pity though, he feels pissed off that he won't get to find out what the temperature's really like in Queensland. Not from Tony anyhow.

The wind blows a small gale at Harry as he makes his way towards the main road and back up the hill. The sun is hidden by clouds but Harry can tell it's getting on. He picks up his speed as best he can. He thinks about Jules and her kid in the pram. The thought creeps in as much as he tries to deny it. Not Jules, but like Jules. He's never followed her, this Jules who is not Jules, the woman that he watches every day. That's the kind of thing that would get a bloke like him locked up. He's thought about it, most days he thinks about it in his desire to know more about her, to know that she's all right. But Harry doesn't like the idea of being locked up and so he makes do with just watching her walk by.

Jules would have made a good mother. The real Jules. He always knew that. Never doubted that. But Harry? He would have made a shit father. How can you be a father if you never had one? How can you know what to do? That's what he'd tell Jules. But Jules would just sigh and shake her head. She never got what he was saying. Never wanted to hear it. Finally he just had to say it. "I don't want kids Jules. Not now, not ever." He'd never really spoken to her like that before and neither of them had anything much to say to each other after that.

He sees now that's when he abandoned her. Swept her feet out from under her and left her sitting alone on her arse. He didn't have a clue what he was doing. Not then, not for a long time after. And Jules? Jules seemed to just get on with it. Took her a bit of time to get her feet back on the ground, but once she did, she just got on with it. And Harry got out of the way.

The mall at the Junction is quiet today. The wind has pushed the browsers and the dawdlers away. Harry pulls his clothes a little tighter together and tells himself he doesn't feel the cold the way other people do. Never has.

It's too early. Harry can tell, it's too early. Nearly time. Nearly. But too early. So he sits on a bench and waits.

Sydney is an expensive city. People flock to Sydney because here you can earn a lot of money. But what Sydney gives with one hand it takes with the other. To survive on nothing but what the government gives her she has learnt to be careful. She controls her money. Nothing is spent without thought and reason. Control, she has decided, is power.

Most of her money goes to pay her rent. The little bit left is for bills, food, travel and extras. It's the extras that have got her interest now. Everything is written down in a notebook. She doesn't need to look in that book to know how much she has in her extras fund. She looks anyway though. It's the rules. And there it is. $40. Enough.

The bookstore is at the bottom of the hill. There are others, bigger, possibly better, a bus ride away but she doesn't think of them. She thinks of the bookstore at the bottom of the hill.

She's spent a lot of time in this bookstore. Never bought anything but spent a lot of time there browsing the shelves, sheltering from the weather. She likes the smell and the feel of the shop. When she is lonely she likes to go there and feel the press of a stranger's body against hers as they negotiate the narrow aisles. Some days she misses the touch of other people. It's been a long time since she's felt two arms around her body, holding her, letting her know she's not alone.

Not that she's some weirdo that puts herself in crowds to feel the touch of others around her. It is not like that. But every now and then, not very often, but every now and then, when she craves the feel of another human body brushing against hers, this is where she comes.

As she strides down the hill, she feels her steps lengthen. She is walking at full speed with great purpose. She sees the publicity surrounding the occasion of her symphony's first public performance. She's wearing black of course, something understated but terribly expensive, possibly a suit. She speaks to the press who surround her, desperate to hear her story. She looks fabulous. She speaks with confidence. She says, "I did it for the man in the bus stop. The homeless man I saw from the bus."

Then she is back on the street. There are no flashing lights, no interested reporters. She is wearing her tracksuit pants and the op shop jumper. She bites her lip. Normally she would change. Normally she wouldn't wear her tracksuit pants out of the apartment. In her excitement to get to the bookshop she has forgotten.

With great effort she brings her attention away from herself and on to the street where she walks. Her step slows. Her stride shortens. She is too close to the bookstore to turn back now. She decides to walk the back streets over the main drag in the hope there will be fewer people to see what she is wearing.

There is a holiday feeling in the air and around the houses. No matter what the weather there is always that holiday feeling here. It's the reason people flock to Bondi. The reason they stay. She can close her eyes and see the suburb in its full summer glory. The crumbling paint on the buildings and the towels hanging over railings and out of windows. She reminds herself of what it feels like to have the sun on her face. And then she opens her eyes and sees she is at the bookstore.

The store is busy. The sheer number of people in the tiny store makes her panic a little. Perhaps someone will find her book before she gets to it. Perhaps they are already on their way to the cash register and she has missed her opportunity.

She starts to squeeze through, pushing her way to the back. She tries to control her panic of not getting there first and enjoy the contact of other people's bodies against hers. Her eyes scan the shelves as she moves. Australian literature on one side, classics next to that. New releases in the middle. Kids books off to the left. Plays and poems hidden in the corner. Pulp fiction in stands all over the place. And then she sees it. It's sitting there on the shelf, waiting just for her. It's in the bargain section, just where she wanted it to be.

The book is not called *How to Write a Symphony* but she realises, now that she's seen the book, that she's not yet ready for how to write a symphony. She needs the book before that. The book in front of her. *The Vintage Guide to Classical Music*. On the cover it says, "An indispensable guide for understanding and enjoying classical music." It is obvious to her now, standing in the bookstore flicking through the pages of the book, that she needs to understand classical music before she can write it. It's the first step. There in her hands, the first step.

She lingers a little while. Her eyes scanning the shelves in case she's missed something but she soon realises there's no point. The book she has in her hands is the book she came to buy so she takes it carefully to the cash register and places it on the counter.

When a bag is offered she refuses. She wants to feel that book in her hands all the way home. This is a mistake, she realises a moment later, as she steps out into the rain. She places the book under her jumper and the receipt carefully into her wallet. The book will become a tax deduction when she sells her symphony for the world to hear.

The first man doesn't much want to talk so he pretends like he hasn't heard Harry and hurries on his way. The second man, he's a little younger and he wants to appear cool, calm, in control and unafraid, so when Harry stands in front of him and says, "What's the time exactly?" the young man stops and listens and then he takes his mobile phone from his pocket and tells Harry that it's ten minutes past ten o'clock.

The next person is a woman and she tells Harry that it's seven minutes past and Harry believes her more than the young man because she's wearing a watch and Harry trusts watches more than he trusts mobile phones. The next person, another woman, this time clutching a baby instead of a briefcase, holds her child like she's afraid Harry will rip it from her and can only shake her head as she moves away.

Harry doesn't care. He moves on to three school kids, all in uniform. They look at their watches; two of them agree that it's 10:15 but the other says 10:13 and an argument ensues as to who's correct. Harry leaves them to it and walks on to the next person pondering on how five minutes could disappear so quickly.

But there's no one to move on to. For a moment it feels as if the mall is deserted. Just Harry and the three school kids arguing among themselves as they move on towards the train station. Harry stands still, waiting, trying to count the seconds, because sometimes on quiet days he likes to try and guess what the time will be next time he asks. But the next person doesn't have a watch and instead he tries to give Harry money. Harry doesn't want money. Not now. He wants to know the time. Exactly. The person behind the money giver tells him it's 10:30. It's a disappointing time.

Harry never believes round numbers. Most people aren't bothered to say it's 10:29 or 10:31. Harry tries to explain to them that he needs to know the time exactly but they still round up or down. Forward or back. A lot of them have those watches without numbers, watches where you can never tell what the time is exactly.

Next is a woman who reminds Harry of a grandmother. Not his grandmother because he can't really remember what his grandmother looked like, but just the type of woman who should be a grandmother. Who looks the way he thinks a grandmother should. She tells him it's 10:35 and he is torn because it seems like a round number but a grandmother wouldn't lie about a thing like the exact time.

After the grandmother-looking woman has blessed him and wandered away, there is another break. Harry uses the time to walk to the other side of the mall. He knows people move to this side of the mall to avoid him. Some people don't want to be stopped and asked what the time is exactly. Most people see him and think he's asking for money. They're the people who cross to the other side of the street when they see the charity collectors too. But Harry isn't asking for money. He just wants to know the time, exactly, and, Harry believes, once people understand that they won't mind telling him. But Harry's wrong. Because most people are on that mall to get where they're going, to get something done. And they don't want to be stopped by a bad-smelling man who insists on being told the exact time, to the minute, to the second, if possible.

Today there isn't anyone on the other side of the mall either. The cold wind, the light rain starting to fall, is keeping everyone away. Harry feels like a lone explorer on an arctic land until someone darts out of a shop. Harry has to run after him as best he can, hunt him down, shouting after him, until the man darting shouts back that it's 11 o'clock and when Harry hears that he is relieved because it's time to head back to the beach.

It is ridiculous. She knows that. Her musical skills don't extend past a shonky version of *Für Elise* she learnt around the age of ten. Her knowledge of musical theory relies on the fact that Every Good Boy Deserves Fruit and All Cows Eat Grass. So it is ridiculous. She acknowledges that. But impossible? She doesn't think it's impossible.

She knows the difference between a sharp and a flat. A major and a minor. She knows how to play a simple chord and a few scales. For the rest she has the book. It's a good start. She'll learn.

She quickly chops the ingredients for a soup and when it's bubbling on the stove it is time for the book. She wants to read it from cover to cover so she starts at the copyright page and then moves on to the table of contents.

Halfway through the first chapter, the book is creating more questions than answers. She has to keep turning to the glossary at the back. Not once but over and over again. And it's not because there are new words being thrown at her, it's the same words, they come so fast and are so unfamiliar that she forgets what they mean. Even when she reads the glossary she still doesn't really understand. So she goes back and forth, back and forth, hoping that if she keeps reading the definitions she will understand the difference and importance of monophonic, polyphonic and homophonic.

As she stands to stir the soup she looks for a piece of paper and a pen. She needs to write it all out. To make notes as she reads. She starts to think about what else she will need to write her symphony. Music. She needs to be able to listen to the music mentioned in the book. But $15 in the extras fund is not going to cover this. She needs alternatives to buying CDs. The library. Second hand CDs at the market. The radio.

At least she has a radio. It's a small black three-in-one. The cassette player stopped working a while back but the radio and the CD player work fine. She stoops to pick it up off the floor, where it's been resting, hidden from view, and she positions it on the kitchen bench. After some time spent turning the dial, she finds music. The music comes out sounding thin and cheap, a little crackly, but it's music. And it's classical. She leans against the wall and closes her eyes. She listens to the curves of the music, the different instruments entering and leaving like it's a busy room.

She starts to make a list. On one side of the paper she writes a heading, "Music I need to hear." On the other side she writes "More things" because she doesn't yet know what they will be.

A second piece of paper is needed to start writing out the terms she doesn't understand. Even as she writes them she has trouble understanding. She starts to feel defeated. Already it's become too much. She feels a sense of dread and disappointment as she stands to stir the soup again. She takes a few breaths. Her father always encouraged her to breathe. It helped then. It helps now. Then she tells herself it's the first day. All she has to do is read the book. She doesn't have to write a symphony today. She just has to read the book.

The soup is ready. She eats. She breathes. She goes back to the book.

Her father loved music. He used to say he was never given the opportunity to learn it. His parents didn't have the money. Then he married young. He had children young. There was never any time for music. But he listened to it all the time. He tried to encourage his children to play. He would sit beside them sometimes to hear them play. One day she walked in to find him at the piano, one of the beginner books in front of him. His fingers poised over the keys. He was embarrassed to be caught and refused to play for her. She laughed when she first saw him. It was a funny thing to see. Now she feels sad for him. Sad that he didn't have the courage to play or the chance to learn. She thinks it will please him, her desire to write a symphony.

She returns to the book. The rain against the building keeps her still, the soup keeps her warm and comfortable and she spends the day on the couch, reading, eating soup, writing out definitions she still can't quite understand.

After clock watching Harry is free and can wander as he pleases. There's always plenty to look at on the way to the beach. A bit of furniture out on the street, an old television or computer. Often a bin or two to rummage in. Harry still worries sometimes when he sorts through a bin. People don't like to see other people looking into their bins. They think it's stealing.

Today Harry finds a jumper. It's a nice woolly one with all different colours and not many holes. Nice and thick and pretty dry. Harry takes off his coat and puts the jumper on then and there. It feels a little tight but Harry figures that'll only make him warmer.

There are not many people at the beach today on account of the weather. Not many gulls either. There is a figure though, huddled up on one of the benches facing the angry looking ocean. As Harry moves closer he recognises the figure as Tony. He's staring out at the water with his shoulders hunched up against the wind. In one hand he's holding chips, all wrapped up in paper, in the other he's got a bottle. He looks clean and like he's wearing new clothes. Even his black, thinning hair looks clean, which is pretty unusual for Tony. The wind has caught Tony's hair and is tossing it about. It reminds Harry of the gulls' feathers after a bit of a fight.

Tony jumps at the sound of Harry approaching. He tenses his grip around the bottle he holds and pulls it close to his body. "Ease up Tone mate, it's only me." Tony's body relaxes but his grasp on the bottle stays firm. Harry makes himself comfortable.

Tony doesn't want to talk. Harry can see that. Tony doesn't even want to look at him.

Silence is fine by Harry. Harry can go whole days without talking to anybody. He can even clock watch without talking. A great show of exaggerated mime and not something he does often. But he can. He can spend a whole day inside his head. It makes him feel clean, not talking for a day or so. Lonely, but Harry doesn't care about that, he always feels lonely anyway and he doesn't often get the chance to feel clean.

They sit out most of the day staring at the grey ocean in front of them. Tony swigs from his bottle until it's gone, then swigs a few more times just to make sure before he throws it to the side. The chips are long gone, he shared a couple of those with Harry. Harry took them gratefully, sure they were a sign that conversation would be coming soon. Harry starts pulling at his new jumper. It's tight under the arms and starting to feel scratchy.

Finally Tony turns to Harry. "Sorry I didn't share me bottle."

Harry shakes his head. "You know I don't touch that stuff." Tony gives a snort of disbelief but Harry lets it go. Tony looks in a bad way and Harry doesn't want to make it worse. Harry feels the cold from the seat creep through his clothes and get under his skin. He's wondering how long he'll be able to stay. He's thinking actually a swig from that now empty bottle might have kept the cold away a bit. If he touched that stuff, which he doesn't.

"I hear the cops got you." Harry says it more to take his mind off the cold and the jumper than because he wants to know about Tony and the cops. Tony just nods. "Bastards," says Harry, thinking his arse is about to go numb and actually a drink is definitely the thing that would have saved him. He watches the gulls and the ocean and the few brave souls who have ventured out for a run along the prom.

"I coulda been in Queensland by now." Tony finally comes out with it, only Harry's barely listening. He's carefully removing his jacket. The new jumper has to go, he doesn't care how warm it is. He takes it off and uses it as a buffer on the seat hoping it will take some of the cold out of his arse. It's a relief to have it off. He feels like he can breathe again. And now that he can breathe again he's starting to think about where he's going to find a meal.

"I coulda been in Queensland by now." Tony starts nodding like his head's agreeing with his mouth and Harry says "yeah" wondering if another "bastards" would be appropriate. He's not sure it is so he sticks to "yeah." Says it again and adds a nod of his own head to match Tony's. Harry tries to make himself believe that Tony could have made it. Maybe he did believe it. Before he saw Tony down here clutching that bottle like it was sunshine, maybe he did.

By sunset Harry's tired of sitting with Tony and all he wants is to be back in his bus shelter waiting for the sound of that creaking pram to tell him it's a new day. But he needs to eat. He leaves Tony still sitting on the bench, staring out at the ocean, and heads towards the main road.

The sun sets fast on the beach. It slips behind the buildings and then it's gone, leaving the night long and cold in front of him. Lights are already going on as Harry starts walking up the main road. The last of the daytime traffic is making its way home. Office workers step from buses and walk quickly towards their homes. Coming the other way are the first evening workers heading out for the night shift. The first theatre, pub and movie goers all heading for buses or waving at taxis. And then the ones like Harry, the first people out looking for something to eat.

Harry knows the people at the Vietnamese restaurant further up the hill. They're good people in that restaurant. Harry can walk in at the end of the night and they'll give him a big serve of food in one of their takeaway containers. They put it in a bag with a napkin and a pair of disposable chopsticks. Harry always gives the chopsticks back. He pulls out the fork he carries in the pocket of his coat to show them and they smile and nod and take back their chopsticks. After Harry has finished eating and used his napkin in a way that would make his mother proud, he carefully washes out the container so that he can return it to them the next day.

Harry likes the people at the Vietnamese restaurant and he would like to visit them now but it's too early to be knocking on their door. It doesn't matter how nice they are and how well they treat him, he knows it's too early to be knocking on their door. So he walks past the restaurant and all the way to his bus shelter and lies down there with his stomach screaming hunger at him. He promises himself he will get up in a little bit and head down the street, maybe to the Vietnamese, maybe to see what's been left in the bin outside the fast food place.

But when Harry wakes up it's to the sound of rain and the feeling that morning is not far away. The rain is not a light sprinkle, it's a pouring, flooding rain. He lies still for a while and listens to the sound of it, knowing it means he'll be waking up hungry and probably without hearing the squeak of the pram wheels. It makes the day bad before it's even begun.

The book is heavy and sometimes awkward to hold as she flicks to the glossary and back. But she has come to love the book. She has come to live in its world. A world where lives were lived for music, through music. A world of people who worked for Dukes and Kings and Churches – all for the purpose of creating music.

She is inspired by the hardships they endured. The children born and lost. Their status as servants. She finds herself understanding the creation of music as a pure act. An act born out of desire that has little to do with greed. It seems that people were born into music in the past. She wonders if this is still the case. And if her task will be impossible simply because she was born into the wrong family.

There are chapters at the end of the book on recent composers. She is keen to get there. Waiting to discover if it is now possible to come to classical music late. Or if still, even today, you must be born into music. As she falls asleep she sees herself at the end of the book. A sombre black and white photo and details of her life. Her late start, her inspiration. Perhaps even a picture of the homeless man sleeping in his bus shelter. And then a picture of her symphony. The notes on a page. She strains her eyes to read the notes. To hear the music that isn't yet there.

The sun rises on another rainy day and still she reads. Still she eats soup. She marks her page carefully and looks at the thickness of the book. She is only up to Mozart. There is a long way to go. She tries to remember back to other composers but it is Mozart who remains in her mind. She remembers the film.

Remembers hearing the actor laugh a crazy laugh. The book says not everything that is in the film is true but she can't help picturing Mozart as that actor, laughing his crazy laugh.

She forces her memory backwards, trying to turn the composers into individuals in her mind. Before Mozart there was Haydn. The one they call the father of the symphony. She likes the look of Haydn. Likes the idea of him being a father. But before Haydn? She can't remember. Can't remember where Handel and Bach and Vivaldi fit in. She can't remember who the grumpy one was.

So she dresses and walks quickly to the library, her book clasped in her hands, her money in a small bag strung across her body from shoulder to opposite hip. Her umbrella struggling against the rain and wind.

At the library she takes her coins to the photocopier and takes copies of the composers' faces. She takes her copies, her book and her bag home again and spends a few hours with scissors and sticky tape. She makes notes around the pictures. Small clues to remind herself who these men were and why they are important to her symphony.

When her pages up to Mozart are finished, she sticks them to her walls. Next to the toilet she sticks a list of definitions. When she looks around the room the faces of the composers start to feel like a crowd and she thinks she might have to go out for a while. She has never been good in large crowds. She stares at the faces. Are they encouraging, sneering? She can't tell. Perhaps they are just watching. She puts on another jumper and leaves the flat.

The day gets worse when Harry feels the rain starting to soak through his blanket and his coat and every other layer he's got on. He gets up quickly and rolls his blanket as small as he can, hoping the smaller he makes it the drier it will stay. He ignores the fact that it's already too wet to be of any use for the next day or two.

Harry looks up at the lightening sky. The rain shows no sign of letting up so he decides to head for the train station. Harry figures it's the best place to be on a day like today. As he walks the rain continues to pour. It soaks through his clothes until he can feel it running rivers down his back. His hair, normally a large grey mass, sticks close to his head and falls wet and dripping in front of his eyes. Harry is shaking by the time he reaches the station. He concentrates on putting one foot in front of the other and tries to think about warm things. Hot summer days. Or big fireplaces. It doesn't make him feel warm but it does get him into the station. Once he's there he stops for a while and lets the rain drip from him and onto the floor.

It's still early. Too early for clock watching. A trickle of people are moving through the station, shaking out umbrellas or coats. Everyone looks cold and miserable. There is no delight in a winter rain, no laughter, no running. Just solemn trudging on as people move from one place to the other. Harry shakes as much water from his head as he can and heads for the toilets to try and dry off.

The toilet has paper towels and an air dryer but the air from the dryer comes out weak and tired. Harry is forced to use the towels as best he can before he heads back out into the station to see if the morning mob has arrived.

Before, when Harry was one of the morning mob, he liked to sneak onto the trains. Even with a valid ticket in his pocket, Harry still liked to sneak in. It's not so easy now. There are automatic gates and people watching, cameras watching, but Harry still likes to give it a go and usually he's successful. It's all in the feet. Watching the feet of the person in front of you, never taking your eyes away from their feet, and moving quick. Once past those gates Harry can spend the day riding the trains, going anywhere he pleases, so long as he doesn't get off. And the inspectors don't get him.

Today the mob is not an office mob and that's how Harry knows it's Saturday. Moving towards the automatic gates are a group of teenage kids. They are absorbed with each other, laughing, talking. They hardly notice Harry slipping in among them as they move through.

Once Harry is on the train platform he waits for clock watching. It's different in a train station. People are standing still. Sometimes they act like they can't hear Harry, even though he repeats himself, even though he's standing right there in front of them, they act like he's invisible. Sometimes, if they can't manage to look through him, they move away. Mostly they tell him the time. They look at their mobile phones. Harry sees that the world has changed since he's been sleeping on the streets. Even the school kids are starting to have mobile phones.

It's warmer down in the station and Harry feels the water start to disappear from him. He watches the station clock. The second hand pushes the minute hand until the hour hand clicks into place and once they're all pointing in the right direction, Harry starts. He starts with the person standing next to him. A man in full suit and raincoat even though it's the weekend.

The man is reading his paper when Harry says to him in a clear voice, "What's the time exactly?"

The man in the suit doesn't want to tell Harry the time. He shuffles a little further away and keeps his eyes on his paper. Harry follows him, moving closer than he was before. He speaks a little louder in case the man didn't hear. "What's the time exactly?" The man continues to read his paper until Harry has to repeat the question three times. He then glances up at the station clock and tells Harry that it's ten o'clock. Harry shakes his head. "What's the time exactly?" The man begins to look nervous, he looks around to make sure there are other people watching and quietly gets out his mobile phone. He tells Harry that it's 10.03 and then he quickly puts his phone back in his pocket. He doesn't go back to reading his paper. Instead he keeps his hand in his pocket. He keeps a check on his possessions and an eye on Harry. But Harry isn't paying any attention to the man in the suit any more. He's moved on to the next person.

A woman. A woman who could be 30 or 50. Harry can't tell. He admires her legs though. Harry's always appreciated a good pair of legs and this woman, she knows she has good legs. It's because of her good legs that she's chosen to wear a skirt, even in this weather. The woman with the nice legs doesn't hesitate to answer Harry's question. She checks her watch. Harry likes her even more. She tells him that it's 10.03 a.m. and Harry really does feel, just for a moment, that time has stood still. He would like to be still for a moment. To savour the feeling of stillness with this woman. But there is a job at hand for Harry and there are two men nearby, standing together. Chums who've been out together the night before. They've had a few laughs together, drunk a few beers, told a few lies and now they are heading for more of the same today. One of them tells Harry that it's 10.07. He says something after that as well. It makes his friend laugh.

Harry doesn't hear. He's been distracted by the noise of an

incoming train. The train makes the people at the station move as one. They crowd around the doors and part as others come flying out of the train and up the escalator. Then the crowd moves on and they disappear into the train. More come running down the escalator and into the train. Then the doors shut, the train moves away and the station is empty. Quiet.

There's just one poor soul who was too slow down the stairs. Who tried to make the train by rushing down the escalator only to realise halfway down it wasn't going to happen. One poor soul who now finds themselves late for the rest of their day. And Harry. The poor soul tells Harry that it's 10.09 and then he paces up and down the platform in the hope it will bring the next train faster.

Harry takes a position at the bottom of the escalator. He watches people descend towards him and as soon as they are within hearing distance he asks, "What's the time exactly?" They tell him 10.12, 10.14, 10.18. And then there's another train. This time Harry places himself in the thick of it all and as the people getting off push past him, Harry asks his question. "What's the time exactly?" But the people are in a hurry and mostly the people don't hear. If they do hear they know they're in an easy position to ignore him. They get on with their day. They don't have time to stop and tell the time to a man who is in need of some new clothes and a good shave.

At the end of the crowd come the stragglers, the ones who aren't in a hurry. The ones who can no longer hurry. One of these, a young man with bad skin and worse breath tells Harry it's 10.20.

The train station starts to get stuffy. Harry gets tired and finds it hard to breathe. He sits on the cold tiled floor and calls to people as they pass, "What's the time exactly?" People walk around him. They don't feel they need to answer his question now that he's sitting and they can avoid him. Harry asks his question in a louder voice. Another train arrives and leaves. Then another. And another. It's been too long between answers and he needs to know the time, exactly. Panic edges into his voice, into his question and finally a man approaches, not too close, but close enough for Harry to hear him. 10.57 the man says to him as he moves to get on a train. These numbers give Harry the courage he needs to stand, to walk to another person and to say, "What's the time exactly?" And she, a young mother who stands with her family, the only one left at the station who wants to talk to Harry, tells him it's 11.03. Harry sighs an audible sigh of relief because it's time to stop and time to catch the next train.

When the train arrives Harry waits, away from the mob, until most are on the train. Then he walks in and takes a seat next to a young bloke. The young bloke has a ring through his eyebrow. Harry stares at him. He looks such a young, clean man. Not the type to have a ring through his eyebrow. He looks nervous too. Harry smiles at him, tries to reassure him with his smile, but the young bloke looks out the window even though the train is travelling through a tunnel and there is nothing to see. Harry takes the opportunity to study the ring. It goes in real deep through his skin. Harry would like to turn it through the skin, to feel if this is an easy thing to do.

His hand reaches out. He doesn't even realise he's doing it. Harry watches as if it's someone else's dry, rough-looking hand, reaching out towards this fresh young skin. The young bloke turns quickly to see Harry's hand in mid-air coming towards him. He stares for a moment, at the hand, at Harry, then he stands, pushes past Harry's knees and walks up the stairs. He stands at the door like he's going to get off at the next station only he doesn't. Harry watches him standing there. Still looking nervous.

The young man with the eyebrow ring gets off a few stations later but Harry sits on that train for hours. He dozes a little, scouts the carriage for food or anything useful and then he looks out the window and sees that the rain has stopped. Harry gets off the train and goes for a walk. He doesn't know where he is. Doesn't even look at the name of the station. Just gets off because it's not raining and because he can.

Harry walks past a row of shops. He moves into streets with only houses. Houses that all look the same and then houses that are different. Houses with gardens and houses with weeds. There are hardly any people, a couple of birds calling overhead and lots and lots of houses.

Soon, his back is sore and his calves are aching. His head feels heavy on his neck. It starts to drop forward, like it wants to be on the ground. But his eyes, they stay open and his legs, they keep walking. Even when they start to shake, they still keep walking.

Harry has done this before. Searched strange suburbs. Walked every inch of them, back and forth. In the beginning he was searching for Jules. For a glimpse of Jules. After he was certain she'd moved from their flat to something larger, more affordable. Something to the west or north. Something with a small yard near a good school. Perhaps something near her parents. He's fairly sure she had parents. Somewhere in the west or north. He's almost certain they weren't in the south.

Suddenly it's dark and Harry thinks maybe he's just going to be walking through the night. He wants his bus shelter. He wants to stop. He doesn't know where he is or how to get back. But he keeps walking. There is nothing else to do. He walks until he can't remember anything else.

Harry wakes just as it's getting light. He drags himself to his feet and starts walking again. Everything is sore and Harry is damp all over. It doesn't stop him. He wants to get back to the beach, back to his bus shelter.

Eventually he finds a train station. There aren't many people at the station and no one is checking tickets so Harry has no problem slipping onto the train. At the Junction, Harry doesn't hide. He doesn't try to sneak back in. He reaches the top of the escalator and then he runs screaming through the gates. People stare but no one stops him.

He sits on a bench in the mall near the station and tries to get his breath back. At least he feels like he can breathe now. Like he's home even though he's yet to see his bench or the ocean. When Harry feels he has sufficient breath he starts to shout at passing people, "What's the time exactly?" There aren't many people. The ones that do pass look at their feet. Sometimes they look at Harry but if they tell him the time, Harry doesn't hear them, he's too busy shouting, "What's the time exactly?" Harry watches the people shuffle past him. He sees them puffed up with the importance of their lives but Harry knows all that importance is rubbish and these people do nothing really that makes any difference.

They make him laugh, these people moving on with their lives, feeling so special and important when Harry knows they're all useless. Harry laughs and laughs. He laughs so hard he finds it hard to shout and when he does start shouting he finds he's no longer asking his question, instead he's shouting, "Stupid fucking people!" and the people walking past all look away and walk a little faster.

Harry stands up and starts walking around a bit. Now he's shouting, "What's the time, stupid fucking people?" Harry watches them trudge past him, one by one, two by two, "Stupid fucking people," he mutters.

And then it becomes a lost day. There's nothing he can do about it. He knows that from experience. Harry has had a lot of experience with stupid fucking people, a lot of lost days. So Harry moves to a different part of the Junction and he stands on a corner with his hat out and his head down and he waits.

Normally, Harry doesn't drink. Never touches the stuff. It's the death of you if you drink on the streets. That's what

Harry says and he says it so often he believes it. Harry doesn't drink. He gave it up. But today is ruined. Destroyed by the stupid fucking people and Harry needs for the day to go away. He needs for it to be tomorrow. One day won't be the death of him. One day doesn't make that much difference.

So Harry stands on the corner with his hat out and his head down and he waits. The money is slow to come but he doesn't need much and eventually he has what he needs. He heads towards the beach and towards the pub. And all the while that Harry waits and all the time that Harry walks, he blames the stupid fucking people.

Booze in hand Harry goes to the beach and finds some like-minded blokes. They look a miserable lot and he doesn't know any of them by name. But he doesn't care because these blokes are holding a couple of bottles in brown paper bags just like Harry and Harry needs someone to talk to. The ocean is dark and wild, the seagulls huddled and quiet. Harry doesn't watch them. Doesn't stare out at the water to spot the surfers, brave or foolish to be out on a day like this. He sits himself down and he starts to tell that miserable group of men about the stupid fucking people. A couple of them nod their heads like they understand what he's saying and Harry takes a big long sip from his bottle. And another. Then he starts to smile as he feels the lost day slipping away.

The ocean is busy, moving quickly into shore. She thinks the sea air will clear her head. She sees him at the park near the beach. He's sitting in one of the rundown picnic shelters with a group of men who look as rough as her homeless man. Some rougher. They drink from bottles in brown paper bags. She sees her homeless man drink from a brown paper bag. She feels a great sense of disappointment that she can't explain. Of course he's no saint. She didn't expect him to be. And public drinking. Well who hasn't done a bit of public drinking? Maybe not from a paper bag but it's the same kind of thing when you think about it.

It's seeing him in a crowd, that's what it is. She imagined him alone, needy. Needing something and she was going to give it to him. Something of his own. Yet here he is surrounded by others. Perhaps he doesn't need her music after all.

She turns away from the men drinking and heads up over the headland. She walks past the golf club and to the streets where there are houses instead of apartments. Where people have space for a garage and a front yard. It feels like a foreign land.

She recalls the image of the homeless man in the bus shelter. She sees him there, huddled on the bench, sleeping through the rain and the traffic. She feels his need for a symphony strengthen inside of her and she turns back towards home, carefully avoiding the section of beach where she saw the group of men drinking.

Back in her apartment she tries to settle on the couch with the book. She reads about Beethoven until she realises her eyes are just following the words. There is no understanding, just words. She leaves the book to go and stand at her balcony. The sky is dark. She can't remember when it turned to night but she understands that it's time to go to bed.

Before sleeping she looks around the room. The pictures of the composers are grey on the walls. They seem familiar now. Less oppressive than they did earlier. Everything else is in its place, everything is as it should be, but something has changed. She looks again. Then she sees the ghosts.

They flit gently about the room. First one, then two, then more. A grand piano appears. The room of course has no space for a grand piano. One of the legs ends up in the kitchen, the other through the couch. The ghost composers take turns to sit at the piano. They listen to each other's music. Some sing as others play. She strains forward to hear their music but they play silently, sing silently, talk, laugh, silently.

In the morning she rises early and checks for any trace of the ghosts, any proof that it was not a dream. Of course she finds nothing. She laughs at herself for even checking. On the couch lies the book and looking at the book she sees that there is not enough to be learnt in that book. She makes an immediate and drastic decision. She sees no other choice. It's time to get a job.

Not just any job of course. But a job around music. A job where she is exposed to music. Where she is around people who understand music. Who love music. She needs money to buy music. To fill her life with music. She needs money to buy tickets to concerts. Or better yet, a job that will give her access to concerts.

She thinks about how to construct her CV while she eats a bit of dry toast, scraped lightly with Vegemite because she's used up all her butter. She already knows what she needs to do. She knew as soon as she made the decision to get a job that she needs to see her brother. She just needs to convince herself there's no other choice before she starts moving. When she's thought through all of the options and is convinced there isn't any other way, she prepares herself to go and see Mark.

Mark, who got the dark, curly hair and darker eyes, while she was left with the kind of brown, nondescript eyes and hair. Mark, who has all the equipment and all of the know-how, and is, she knows, nice enough to help her. There'll be questions of course. Questions she doesn't want to answer and ones perhaps she won't be able to answer. But there is no escaping the fact that she needs to see Mark.

She dresses quickly and heads to the door. Before leaving she sees movement in the shadows. She stops to look. The movement has frightened her a little. It's probably just the light moving, a bird flying outside. She checks for ghosts. She tells herself there are no ghosts but she checks for ghosts anyway. Then she leaves. There are other things to worry about now.

The bus to Mark's house is slow with little that interests her on the way. She spends the time thinking about Mark. The last time she saw him was his birthday party. She arrived late. Had an excuse ready about another event when in fact she was late because she didn't have the money to pay for dinner. Didn't want to sit with his friends who are all so sure of themselves.

She plans what she will say to Mark. She will just say she needs a job. That she's sick of the dole. They were never close as siblings. Never a family to share secrets and dreams. They both did their best when she first moved here. Him more than her. He tried to include her in his social circle, show her around a bit. But neither of them kept it up. They drifted away from each other the same way they drifted away from each other when they lived at home. No more than a polite interest in each other's lives. At least they were polite. At least she still feels she can ask him for help. It's only when she is standing at his door at seven in the morning that she realises how early it is, how she should have called first.

The door opens before she can knock and one of his housemates walks out to see her standing there. He says, "Hey…" in a way that means he remembers her but can't remember her name. She doesn't care. She can't remember his name either. So she answers. "Hey." He says, "You here to see Mark?" and all she has to do is nod which is so much easier than having to ask. He says, "He's still in bed," and stands aside to let her in before shouting at the closed door on the left. "Mark, you've got a visitor." Then he smiles and says, "See you," and she says, "Yeah, see you," surprised that he is being so nice.

Mark appears about the time she starts thinking about quietly leaving. He smiles a sleepy smile when he sees her and she feels relieved. He sets her up in the kitchen with a cup of coffee and then heads for the shower. Another figure emerges from Mark's bedroom to join him in the shower. She sits drinking her coffee. She tries to conjure music in her head so that she doesn't have to hear the noises in the bathroom and then, when the music in her head falls quiet, she begins to think about leaving again.

It feels like a good hour before Mark has himself together and the girl has left. By then she has surrendered. She doesn't care if Mark asks her questions. She doesn't care if he doesn't understand. She just wants the CV. She sees, in that hour, how much she wants the CV, how her desire for the CV helped her to stay. She asks without hesitation, she asks with an urgency that suggests she is running out of time, though it is more that she just wants to leave. He doesn't ask her why and she is grateful. He raises his eyebrows, he mutters, "Classical music," to himself, and then he heads for his computer.

Mark is an excellent liar because Mark doesn't lie. He uses truth in a strange way, a way others may not think to, but he doesn't outright lie. Through Mark's fingertips on the keyboard her two years of working for the local video store, her six months in the mail room of an accounting firm, her café work, her failed film career and all of her other half-finished pursuits become the reasons why she is the perfect candidate for work. Low-level customer service or admin work. But still, work.

The printer moves into action. They stand silently side by side and watch the pages emerge. She'd like to tell Mark what she's doing. She'd like to see him impressed by the scale of her project. But she is afraid. If she says the words will that be it? Will that be enough just to say what she is going to do? Perhaps then she'd never actually do it? Then life would return to the way it was before she saw the homeless man from the bus, before she bought the book, before she saw the ghosts. She doesn't want that.

So she stays quiet.

The printer stops. She holds the still fresh pages and kisses Mark quickly on the cheek to thank him, then wonders if she should have. If she's taken a step too far, too close. He says, "You should stop around more," as they head to the door. She says, "Yeah, ok." He says, "Give me a call," as she steps onto the street and then, "Let me know how you get on." She says, "Sure," and thanks him again. She waves her new CV at him as he watches her walk towards the city.

It's a little after nine when she makes it to the employment agency. She walks in to see a number of people already waiting before her and wishes she'd brought the book. That she had thought ahead. The receptionist tells her the wait will be an hour and she tries to smile to show that she is accommodating and flexible. That she is employable. She says "That's no problem," and looks for a seat.

The wait ends up being an hour and a half. She tries to maintain her smile that whole time. Inside she begins to feel defeated. Nervous. The agent looks carefully over her CV. Turns it over to the blank page on the back to see if there's anything else. The agent asks her, "What have you been doing since your last job?" and she is prepared for this question. She tells him she's been working on personal projects. Creative projects. He nods, looking unconvinced. She suppresses the urge to say more. Less is more she has decided. Smile, look keen, look willing. Try not to speak too much.

The agent isn't that interested in her. She can tell by the way he slowly turns to his computer. The way he doesn't look at her, doesn't chat with her. She understands she is not a good money making prospect for this agent. But still she smiles. Still she tries to look keen and willing.

He says, "Can you type?" and "Have you ever worked in an office before?" He says, "Most people have certificates for office work now. Have you thought about doing some study?" She talks about the accountancy mail room. How they gave her lots of different jobs. How some of it was computer work. How she doesn't have one at home but she knows how to use one. How she used one at school. How she's quick to learn.

He says, "Why did you leave your last job?" She tells him she left for study. She starts to talk about how the study didn't work out the way she wanted but she trails off. Telling him that would be telling him she never actually made it to the study. He isn't interested. She is talking too much.

The agent sighs and rubs his chin with his hand. He tells her there's nothing at the moment but that something might come up. He asks her, "Will you take something that isn't music related?" and she wants to say no but she doesn't. She says that she's open to any opportunities. She thinks that's what she should say. But she wants to say no.

Her answer seems to satisfy him. He nods his head and says, "I'll call you if anything turns up."

There's not much conversation after Harry's spiel about the stupid fucking people. Harry doesn't care. He's starting to forget about the stupid fucking people as he looks out at the water and watches the gulls. The gulls are dancing today. A fairweather dance. They group and then part. Then group again. They don't squabble because there's no food to squabble over. No one's on the beach except a few blokes with brown paper bags. So instead of fighting, the gulls dance. They hope for sun, for with sun come people and with people comes food.

Harry likes the sun too. He finds the cold gets into his bones. Some days he feels like he's freezing from the inside out. Even when he wears all the clothes he can find, he still feels his bones are cold and no one can feel comfortable with cold bones.

Harry looks up at the sky and watches the wind blow the clouds around. He wonders if it's going to rain. Harry thinks about rain a lot. He thinks about short autumns and early winters. He thinks about wet summers where even though it's warm you can never get dry. He thinks about these things a lot but he knows there's nothing you can do about the weather. Nothing you can do to stop winter coming. Even the gulls, with their fair weather dance, can't stop the rain. If it wants to rain, it's going to rain and there's nothing Harry or the gulls can do about it.

Harry stands up to tell the gulls because it seems they don't understand. He shouts at them, "You can't do nothing about the weather." The gulls stop their dance for a moment and listen to the words that arrive on the wind. They laugh at Harry among themselves and then they start their dance again. So Harry has to shout again because maybe they didn't hear him right. "You can't do nothing about the weather. I should know. I tried once. You can't do nothing about the weather." This time the gulls don't even pause to laugh at him, they just keep dancing.

Harry looks around him and sees that he's alone. His bottle is empty and thrown on the grass, still in its paper bag and looking like yesterday's toy. The other blokes have disappeared. Maybe they said goodbye. Harry doesn't remember. Harry doesn't care.

As a little boy Harry's mother talked a lot about caring. Caring how you looked, caring how you spoke. Caring what others thought of you. Harry sees mothers on the street just the same as his mother was. Always pulling fingers out of kids' noses and pushing them in the back until they say "Thank you." Kieran's mum'll be just the same. She'll slap his fingers if he grabs for something without asking. She'll make him tuck his shirt in when it's hanging out.

But Harry sees now that those things aren't as important as he once was told they were. They aren't the real bad habits. The real bad habits are the things that get you into real trouble. Things that get your job lost, your girlfriend throwing you out of the flat. Those are real bad habits and Harry has got a few of those.

Harry sits a long time watching the ocean and thinking about bad habits. He realises with a small sense of relief that he's stopped thinking about the stupid fucking people. Then he sees that it's dark. That even the seagulls are heading away from the cold of the ocean. He stands. It's time to be getting back to his bus shelter. But then Harry looks up at the sky and he sees there isn't a cloud up there and then he sees the stars start to shine. Even with the glare of the cars and the shops behind him he can see the stars and it looks beautiful. So beautiful Harry decides to lie down for a while and just look.

When Harry opens his eyes again he's lost the stars. He's lost his way. It's dark and cold and he's not sure where he is. He can't hear the ocean, can't hear anything. He doesn't feel uncomfortable though. Sure it's cold, the ground beneath him is like an ice block. But he doesn't hurt anywhere. He feels no pain. And then there's something warm. At first he can't work out where it's coming from. Just something warm that makes him feel good and cosy. It's piss. His piss. Running down his leg. Harry comes to realise this but he doesn't care. It feels good and warm and that's all that matters.

And then there's a voice that ruins it all. "You're an accident waiting to happen, you are." Harry moves his head to try to see where the voice is coming from. "An accident waiting to happen." Harry turns to see boots near his head. Bloody Brian. Harry closes his eyes. He doesn't want to see Bloody Brian just now. Harry opens his mouth to speak but it's all dry and rough and he can't get any words out. Bloody Brian reaches down with his big hairy arms and suddenly Harry is on his feet. Harry stumbles a little until he regains his balance. "An accident …"

"Fuck off." Harry's got his voice back. He feels the last of his piss run down his leg but that warm, good feeling has gone. He tries to focus on Bloody Brian standing before him. He tries to think of a way out of the situation. "I hate me brother *and* me sister." Actually Harry hasn't thought about his brother and sister for a long time but it's the only thing he can think to say. Bloody Brian likes it when you talk. He likes to know what you're thinking. He says it again. "I hate me brother and me sister." If he can keep Bloody Brian talking then perhaps the inevitable can be avoided a little longer.

"Do you mate?" Bloody Brian has Harry by the arm now and is starting to make him walk. He won't be distracted. "You could have died out there tonight mate, you know that?" Bloody Brian isn't standing so close now. He's noticed the piss. But he's still walking Harry. Still leading him on to a place Harry prefers not to go.

"I don't care." They're stumbling up the street now. "That's what's unusual about me. I don't care." Harry collapses his legs in an attempt to sit on the ground. But Bloody Brian is a strong man, much stronger than Harry and he pulls him easily back to his feet. Harry gives in. He walks with Bloody Brian, stumbling along the uneven path, allowing Bloody Brian to do what Bloody Brian feels he was born to do. He calls it helping. Harry calls it interfering.

It feels to Harry like they walk forever with Bloody Brian going on about some bloke called John Howard and how he changed the rules and made all this work for Bloody Brian. How he doesn't have time to be picking Harry up off the ground. Harry doesn't know who John Howard is but he hears his name a bit and it seems like a lot of people are mad at him. He would have thought Bloody Brian would be happy with more work, more people out on the street to save but Bloody Brian seems pretty pissed off about it tonight. Then all too soon they are there. The lights are too bright and the room already stinks like piss and booze and dirty washing. There's something else too. Another smell worse than all those others that Harry can't place. And then he's lying in a bed and Bloody Brian has gone. Harry thinks he'll just lie there a little time and once Bloody Brian has forgotten him, once he's moved on to the next poor bastard, then he'll leave.

Harry wakes up in the shelter. He wakes up stinking and swearing with a head the size of Canada.

SECOND

The ghosts wait until the full darkness of night has arrived. They wait until she has settled into a comfortable sleep. And then they come. One, two, three. More than she can recognise. They argue over who is going to play the piano next and they pat each other on the back, admire each other's music that they were not alive to hear.

Before bed she picked up the book, determined to discover who is who. She wants to be able to walk between the ghosts. To conquer any fear she has of them. To use them. To learn from them. She wants them to guide her as she writes her symphony. A ghost army of mentors.

She wants to ask them, "Do you have to be a child prodigy to be a great composer?" She wants to know, "Where are all the women?" Because so far the book has only talked about men and she's looked at the index and none of the names sound like women. In her dream all of the ghosts, of course, are men. "Where," she asks them, "are the women?"

But the ghosts remain silent. They behave like she isn't there. In their hands she can see paper, sheet music. She tries to take it from them. She wants to see the notes. But the pages are blank. There are no voices, there is no music coming from the ghost piano. She thinks if she can just focus a little harder, concentrate a little more she will be able to hear them. But there is only silence. All they offer her is their presence.

She feels very tired. She didn't know you could feel tired in your sleep. She can't let the ghosts rest. Perhaps they can't let her rest. She stands to shout at them. She says, "I will be the next one. I will be the next one of you." And Beethoven, she's sure it is Beethoven, Beethoven who died deaf and in death finds his hearing restored, he says, "Of course you are. That's why we're here."

She wakes in the morning to the sound of the phone ringing. The sun is bright in the sky and the flat is empty and quiet. It's the employment agent. He doesn't sound pleased to be ringing her. He sounds hurried, impatient. Like he has a list of calls to make. Like she isn't the call he'd like to be making. But he's ringing her. He tells her a music school is in need of a temporary office assistant. That the role would be to perform some sort of stocktake. That it would be every day for at least two weeks. Maybe longer depending on how she works out. Shorter if she doesn't. He says if she wants it she needs to be there in an hour.

She asks him which music school. She is hoping for the Conservatorium. It's not the Conservatorium. It's a music school she knows nothing about. But it's only a bus ride away and it's music and a job. She wants to ask him more questions but he isn't interested in conversation. He tells her if she wants it she needs to get moving. He gives her the address and the name of the person she needs to speak to. He wishes her luck but not in a way that sounds like he means it. He wishes her luck to end the conversation, to hang up the phone.

She feels nervous as she quickly showers and dresses to leave. She isn't sure what to wear. What to bring with her. She takes her book and her bus fare. She puts Vegemite between two pieces of bread and adds that to her bag. She rushes out of the door hoping that her still damp hair will be dry by the time she gets there.

The agent has told her that the school is near Central Station so she catches the bus to Central hoping it will be easy to find. The bus is slow, it hits every red light, stops at every bus stop for people to get on or off. The bus feels slower than usual. The traffic is heavier than she's used to. Despite the cold of the day she starts to sweat from the anxiety of being on the bus, from the worry over finding the school and what she will find there if she does.

The school turns out to be easy to find but the person she is meant to speak to isn't. She stands, in the middle of a busy hall, too shy to ask the students who rush past her. There's no obvious reception. Finally, after considering walking out, going home, she has to force herself to stop someone and ask them, "Where is Deanne Evans? Can you tell me how to find Deanne Evans?" The student she stops is helpful with kind eyes. Maybe the same age as her. Maybe a bit older. He stops and listens to her. Smiles at her. He points her in the right direction and asks if she'd like him to take her. She says no. She wants to say yes. Maybe just to be with his smiling eyes a bit longer. But she says no. She thinks she needs to arrive unassisted. She thinks this will make her seem more capable.

Deanne Evans is older than her by a good decade, maybe two. She is helpful but seems tired. She starts a long explanation about how the job came to be, about why it needs to be done and about why she can't do it herself. Then cuts herself off. She says, "Oh you don't need to know all that." And then she explains the job itself. She wants the long explanation, she wants to know everything about the school, everything Deanne Evans can tell her. She watches the students move past the door of the room they are in and feels a stab of envy. She becomes a little distracted and wonders where they are going, what they are learning. When she brings her attention back to Deanne she realises she has missed a little of what she is meant to be doing.

What she starts to understand about her job is that she is to perform a stocktake of the school's sheet music collection. She is to work through the collection, piece by piece, using a computer to log the presence of each piece. She is to note down any that are not where they should be. As she starts to work, her eyes are drawn to the students again. There seems to be an endless stream of students. Her ears strain to hear music being played further down the hall but the sounds are too muffled by doors and soundproofing.

She tries her best. All morning she tries her best. She wants Deanne Evans to like her so she takes the work seriously. Handles the music with care. Tries not to be too distracted by trying to read it or by the parade of students that pass the door. She wants to do a good job.

At the end of the day, as she walks away from the music school, she thinks about who she could call. She wants to celebrate her first day of working. Blow the $15 she has left in her extras fund. She could call Mark. He said to let him know how she got on. She could call him but then what? Would he ask her questions? Would she have to explain herself? Would she need to tell him that it was more than a job? That there is a purpose underneath the job? Would he really care anyway?

As she sits on the bus she thinks through a list of other people she could call. It seems she is between friends at the moment. She hasn't been going out much lately. Not since she moved to the beach. Hasn't seen many of the people she used to know, hasn't even spoken to them. In the beginning there was an excuse, usually money. Then it just became how she lived. And now, as she sits on the bus, she realises she really is alone. It's not a frightening thought. Not a sad thought. Just a realisation. She's surprised it hasn't properly occurred to her before.

She gets off the bus at the Junction so that she can walk past the bus shelter. She thinks if he is there, perhaps she will tell him. Perhaps he would understand, and if he questioned her, she feels she could explain to him. It means a long walk home in weather that is now unpleasant but it feels important. She wants him to know that she has made an important step towards making his symphony happen.

The wind pulls at her clothes and hair. It tries to get underneath her coat and into her skin. She pulls her coat tighter around her and walks on to the bus shelter, head down, shoulders hunched against the cold wind.

She sees that the bus shelter is empty with a mixture of disappointment and relief. She stands for a while, enjoying a break from the strength of the wind. She doesn't know whether to sit. Whether that would be okay. There is a neat pile of belongings in the corner of the shelter. A few bare blankets and some other things she can't make out. Secrets, hidden among his belongings. Maybe something else to wear or a picture of someone he used to love.

She wants to leave something for him. A calling card so he knows she was here, that she was thinking of him. She looks through her bag. The only food in her bag is an old mint she wouldn't eat herself so she can't give it to him. She looks on the ground. She's feeling a little desperate now. Between the spaces on the footpath there's a small yellow flower. A weed really, whose petals have been damaged by the wind. Still it's something. She places the flower carefully on his pile of belongings and then she struggles against the wind to her home.

That night she dreams of music. Music fills the corners of her apartment and the corners of her. She dreams of music flowing through her body like blood. Her heart pumps the music to her toes, her fingers, to the tips of her hair. She dreams of music exploding from her hands. She dreams of the music school. Of going into the rooms that hold sheet music, records and CDs and eating them all. One after the other. Her fingers pull anxiously at the thin plastic sleeves that protect the records and her hands shake as she pulls open the cases of the CDs. She takes them one at a time. Those she can't eat there and then she hides in her clothing. She'll eat them later.

She wakes hungry, reads her book over breakfast before rushing through the shower. She wants to get to work on time. Early if she can. She quickly packs a simple lunch and puts her book in her bag. Choosing what to wear isn't easy. Her wardrobe isn't big on choice, particularly not work attire. The school seemed pretty casual, half of the students were in tracksuits and Deanne was in jeans but she doesn't feel ready to turn up to work in jeans yet. She's trying to impress. Trying to look professional.

She settles on a version of the same outfit she wore yesterday. She puts her hair up instead of wearing it down. She hopes this is enough to make it look like a whole new outfit.

At the bus stop she examines the clothing worn by the other workers who are waiting with her. She tries to picture herself in these clothes. Would they suit her? Would she look too dressed up? Some of the outfits look expensive. The women wearing them are probably lawyers, high-level accountants. She'd like to look as confident as they do. She's not sure an expensive outfit would be enough.

She purchases a week-long ticket. It uses up the last of her money but she tells herself that this is a cost-effective decision. She tells herself this but she worries. She still doesn't know how long the job will last. Whether they will want her the next day.

The bus moves too quickly past the bus shelter for her to see if he's there. If he found her flower. At first she thinks the bus is going too fast. She thinks she'll have too much time with nothing to do once she arrives. That she will have to sit in the cold of the morning with her book for too long. That she will arrive to work, on time but chilled. Perhaps so chilled that she ends up with a cold and can't work the full day. Can't come back the next day. She expects they would find someone else if that happened. She has not managed to prove her worth yet.

But once through the Junction the bus slows. It hits every red light. It stops at every stop to pick up people, let people off.

It moves so slowly that she starts to panic. She considers getting off the bus. Walking seems faster than the ever-stopping bus. She'd consider catching a taxi but she has no money now that she's bought the weekly bus ticket. She stares out the window, counting lights, counting stops. She tries to concentrate on breathing. One breath after the other. The bus moves slowly on.

In the end she arrives at work perfectly on time and completely panicked. Deanne looks pleased to see her. Pleased that she has shown up again. It eases some of her panic. Before starting work for the day, Deanne offers to show her around the school. They walk the corridors among the students and Deanne points out classrooms and rehearsal rooms and small practice rooms that are only big enough for a piano and two chairs. She shows her where the students eat, where the main theatre is, and where the teachers' rooms are.

She feels lost among the students and corridors. But she is excited too. There is energy in the school. A feeling of possibility that comes from the laughter of the students as they rush past. The small rooms holding only a piano are next to other rooms that hold drum kits or empty rooms, ready for students to bring in their instruments. She wants to sit in those rooms. She wants to touch the piano, put a violin under her chin.

Deanne is less flustered today. She tells her clearly why she's been brought in. How there used to be someone else who worked here who unexpectedly left. How they haven't had time to fill the role but they just had to get the stocktake done. How there's no way she'd have time to do it herself on top of everything else she has to do. The explanation helps. She can see that there are days of work ahead of her if she works hard, turns up on time, tries her best, smiles.

After Deanne has finished her tour and they are back in the room where she is working, Deanne invites her to lunch. It's not really phrased as an invitation she can refuse. It is a further instruction. Deanne will collect her at lunchtime. They will go to the staff room. She will be introduced to other staff members there. Deanne asks her, "Did you bring your lunch or do you need to buy something?" and when she says she brought her lunch with her Deanne nods like she got the answer right.

The morning passes quickly because she works quickly. Secure in the knowledge that there is more work to follow. She sorts through the music, moving from shelf to computer then back to shelf. Her eyes frequently move to the doorway, to the movement of students that pass. Her ears strain to hear the muffled sounds of conversation and music that fill the hall outside of her room.

Anything she is unsure of she piles next to her computer, ready to ask Deanne. When Deanne collects her for lunch, she shows the pile to Deanne who nods again like she got it right and says, "After lunch."

In the staff lunchroom the other staff are polite but not particularly interested. Deanne introduces everyone quickly and she struggles to remember even one or two of the names. They all shake her hand or smile if their hands are full of food or work. But they don't chat. This is Deanne's role.

As she eats her sandwich Deanne tells her about the school. Some of the history, about how it is run now, about how long Deanne has been working there and what she does. She tries to think of questions as Deanne talks. To show her that she's interested, that she wants to hear more. Because she is interested. But she is also nervous, anxious about saying or doing the right thing and this anxiety makes it hard for her to focus on Deanne's words.

She is disappointed when Deanne tells her that there is not a lot of focus on classical music at the school. That the students are more interested in modern forms of music. She finishes her sandwich quickly and drinks the tea Deanne has made for her. She listens and she smiles and she nods and she tries not to be distracted by the other staff or by the conversations of the musicians in the room. When Deanne says that it's time to get back to work she tries to express the enthusiasm she feels. She is coming to enjoy being in that room, by herself, surrounded by music.

After lunch she starts to look more closely at the music in her hands. She sorts the sheet music the way Deanne has told her to and when she finds the classical music, the Beethoven and the Bach and the other composers that she's read about as well as the ones she hasn't got to yet and the ones who didn't make it into the book, she stares at the notes on the page, the complexity of their rhythms and the keys that the music is written in.

She sees their complexity and she sees the enormity of the task that she has set herself but she doesn't feel defeated. She feels excited. Like it is still possible.

The flower on his blankets really throws Harry. It upsets him for days. At first he thinks it means something nice. He thinks maybe it's the woman with the baby, the one he calls Jules. Maybe she really does notice him. Maybe it's someone else. Someone he doesn't know, but someone who cares. Then his thoughts turn darker. Someone's been in his shelter. Maybe they've looked through his stuff. Maybe it's some kind of warning. Harry has never been the type to give flowers. Never been the type to receive them either. He has no idea what it means.

Sometimes he is sensible. The flower is nothing. It means nothing. It was kids making fun or left accidentally. Sometimes he is wishful. Maybe it was Jules. This is the thought at the bottom of everything. The thought he's been trying not to think. Maybe it was Jules. Maybe she found him. Maybe she's always known he was there. Maybe he has been forgiven.

Harry spends days lost in contemplation about this one yellow flower. It takes only a few days for the flower to dry up and crumble away and yet Harry is still sitting there thinking about it. Because even though the flower he was given has gone, dried up, died and returned to dust, those stupid yellow flowers are everywhere. They grow up out of nowhere and they remind Harry that no matter how much time he has spent thinking, wondering, he still does not know why it was there.

Harry starts to kick those little yellow flowers. He stomps on them every time he sees them springing up between the grey concrete of the footpath. He picks and scatters the petals with his hands and grinds the stem away with his heel.

And then Harry lets it go. There are too many flowers, too many questions. He sees that he could let them take control. That this is getting out of control. So he makes an effort to look at the sky instead of the ground. He tries to think about other things and he lets the little yellow flowers go.

Harry sits in his bus shelter and watches the day pass. It seems that every day it gets colder and wetter. Every day the little sun there is, disappears earlier. The people walking by wear more and more clothing. Harry feels the winter crowding around his shoulders. He finds it hard to leave his shelter. He talks himself into believing it will be over soon. He tells himself people wear these coats and then they take them off. The days get shorter and then they get longer again. Winter isn't so bad in Sydney, he tells himself. But all he can see is a long winter stretched before him. All he can see is people in thick, warm coats while his is old and thin.

Harry has lost track of the number of years he's sat in this shelter and watched the world go by. He's seen couples walk together, day after day, and then seen them suddenly walk apart or disappear completely. He's seen a man in a good suit stride past every morning with purpose turn into a bloke in jeans and a t-shirt with a dull expression. Harry knows he's taken this place in the bus shelter from another much like himself. Someone who died in the cold of the night or stumbled without thinking onto the road one morning. He knows that after him someone else will come and take his place. Just like someone probably came and took his job, his flat, Jules.

Today, after he's checked the time at the Junction, and sat in his shelter for as long as he can stand it, Harry walks down to the beach. The ocean is there, moving back and forth across the sand. Sometimes it crashes like it's in a real big hurry to say something important and sometimes it just moves all gentle like it's listening to the gulls. There are a few tourists out today. They brave the cold because they know they have a warm bus waiting for them when they've had enough. Some of them even take their shoes off and put a toe in the water. A wave comes up and surprises them. Wets them to their knees. But they only laugh. Of course they laugh. At the end of the warm bus ride is a warm hotel room and in that room is a suitcase of warm, clean clothes. Why wouldn't they laugh?

There's a couple down near the water too. They're holding hands and acting like the cold doesn't bother them. Couples piss Harry off today. Some days, some rare sunshine days, they make him smile. But today is not a sunshine day. Today is a cold, grey day and today couples piss Harry off.

Harry remembers being part of a couple. He remembers whispering at night, having someone to talk to when he woke up. Not that he's got anything to say now. Or ever. Harry would be the first to admit that he doesn't have anything important to discuss. But he still remembers with a feeling like longing that starts in his legs and settles in his gut, he still remembers having someone there. Someone to listen to him whispering at night.

He remembers after Jules, while he was on the street. He doesn't remember how she came to be there. How she attached herself to him. Maybe he never knew. Maybe she was just there one day. Maybe he attached himself to her. He doesn't remember. But there was someone. He remembers that. Someone who was there when he went to sleep and there when he woke up. Mostly. They used to talk. Talk about anything. She'd tell Harry her dreams. Harry thought they were stupid bloody dreams that didn't make any sense. But he listened. She'd tell him her secrets too.

For a while he liked the company. He told himself at the time that Jules would have liked her. Would have approved of their relationship, such that it was. And then wasn't. But this is probably not true. Jules would not approve of anything Harry's done since they parted and didn't approve of a lot of what he did while they were together. Still, for a while Harry had someone to whisper to in the night. Now and then Harry tries to remember one of her stupid bloody dreams. Just one. He can't. He still remembers a few of the secrets.

Harry brings his attention back to the waves. The tourists have gone, the couple has passed. The gulls huddle together in an attempt to find some protection from the wind. There's nothing for them to fight over today. Harry's cold and tired and hungry but he reckons he's glad to be here at the beach instead of stuck in an office listening to the seconds tick by on the clock hanging high on the wall. He's glad to be staring at the gulls and the roaring ocean instead of a desk with papers he has no interest in and doesn't really understand, trying not to look at the clock because if he did he wouldn't be able to look away and would end up sitting there watching five minutes tick away, second by second. People in offices notice things like that. It doesn't look good, a person who's meant to be working just sitting there staring at the clock. A person could lose their job for that.

The subject she continues to return to is age. All of the composers she reads about, all of the ghosts that have moved from her dreams and are now occupying her flat, they all started young. Child prodigies, or at least very accomplished musicians by the time they reached 20. And here she is at 28. Probably too old for any of this. She realised a while ago that she was never going to be a supermodel. A rock star. Never going to be a great athlete. Unless it is marathon running. That still seems like something she could do. If she started now. She knew all that but she thought there was a lot left she could do. Sure those obvious youth-driven careers are off the table. But she thought there was more. A lot more she could still become. Now she's starting to think that if you don't start young you don't have a chance. That you just have to take whatever you can grab. And that just doesn't seem fair.

Of course there are some things she can do. Things that are not remarkable, noteworthy or world changing but things nonetheless that she can do. Things that she can do with her eyes shut and one hand tied behind her back. Like a music stocktake.

She thought working would be harder. She thought there would be things to learn. Challenges to overcome. She thought there would be moments when she would feel lost and confused. But it's like she was born to it.

She works out the buses and how to arrive early for work every day. She always makes a point of leaving five minutes later than her finish time. Some days she finds it hard to stop. She thinks I'll stop after the next one. And then the one after that takes her attention, so she does that one too. Some days she doesn't want the day to end. She doesn't want to leave to spend another night at home with just the ghosts for company. Their music and chatter still silent to her ears.

She hears music at the school. Sometimes music like the music she wants to write. Mostly music that is nothing like want she wants to write. She sees there is knowledge in the school. In the teachers and in the students. In the books and sheets of music that line the walls, fill the draws. She wants that knowledge for herself. She wants to be able to close her eyes and hear the music, her music, and know how to put it on the page. The longer she listens, the more she reads, the further she feels she is from actually writing anything down. Now she knows a little of what is involved. A little of what she needs to learn. Now she knows how hard it will be.

She curses her parents for not sitting her in front of the piano at age two. She curses them for not forcing her to practise more when they did finally put her in front of a piano. She curses herself for all her faults, too long and various to list.

She continues to read the book like it holds the answers. She reads it while she eats breakfast. She reads it on the bus going to and from work. Sometimes, if Deanne is too busy to have lunch with her, she reads it at work. Not in the staff room where others could see but in the park behind the school. She reads it in bed before she goes to sleep. She'd read it walking down the street from the bus to the school, if she thought she could do it without bumping into strangers or posts.

At work she finds that is acceptable to listen to music while she works. Deanne shows her a small CD player and a stack of CDs. She tells her what a great job she's doing and how she knows how boring it is and how impressed she is that she hasn't given up. She suggests she might want to listen to music while she's working. That maybe this will help the boredom. She tells

Deanne it's not boring for her. That she enjoys it. And Deanne rolls her eyes like she always does, like she doesn't believe her but appreciates the lie.

She starts to listen to music while she works, like Deanne suggested. But when she does it makes the idea of writing a symphony seem impossible. She can barely tell the instruments apart. Barely discern a structure. She has no idea about key, except what she reads on the covers. She feels lost within the music. But she loves it too. When she listens to the Brandenburg Concertos her heart soars. When she listens to Beethoven's 3rd Symphony she knows she can't stop trying. Somewhere inside of her she feels music. Music like Beethoven's. All she has to do is find it.

Her nightly visitors, those ghosts haunting her apartment, start to follow her to the school to watch her work. They abandoned the pretence of only appearing when she was asleep after a few days and now they abandon the rule of staying within the confines of her apartment. At first she told them "No" and "Stay" but they slipped in behind her on the bus. They snuck through the doors and into the room where she works. She's gotten used to having them now, always behind her, around her, shadowing her every move.

The ghosts are excited by the music held magically within those shiny flat discs. They are excited by the presence of real pianos in the small rooms. They count the number of works with their own name and boast to each other about who has the most. She does not question their presence. Does not wonder why they were in her dreams and now she sees them waking. She becomes grateful for the company.

They are still silent. Even in their boasting, they remain silent. All except Beethoven who continues to talk to her. Sometimes she wishes Haydn would speak. She thinks perhaps he would be a little more encouraging. A little more nurturing. If Mozart spoke perhaps life would become a little more fun, perhaps she would care a little less, laugh a little more. But it is Beethoven who talks. He tells her she must do more than just listen to the music. He tells her she needs to play. And she feels it too. She feels it drawing her in, the keys of the pianos in their own little rooms, the seat poised in just the right place, asking her to sit. She walks past those rooms all the time. Even when she doesn't have to. She takes the long way around. Just to look. Often there are students in there. Usually alone, but sometimes with a friend or teacher sitting next to them. Once, when a room was empty, the door wide open, she walked in, gently touched a few of the keys without making a sound.

Harry knows that life is about more than sitting between four walls all day. Coming home so that you can go to sleep so that you can go back to work. Life is more than that. More than money and a nice place to live. But way back Harry was so proud. So proud to have a job. Then to have a job in the city where he was required to wear a tie. So proud. And so scared.

It was only Jules that kept him at that job as long as he stuck at it. Only Jules who made him want to go there; go there so he could come home to her. It was Jules who encouraged him to try for that promotion. And that, Harry has decided, that is when it all went wrong.

Rain starts to fall and Harry shakes it from his head and clothes as if it's regret and forces himself to remember happier times. He remembers how they danced in the rain. How Jules looked at him and yelled "Bucketing!" because the rain was getting heavier and heavier but still they danced. Later, days, weeks, months later when they were warm and dry Jules said they danced because they were pissed but Harry knew it was because they were happy.

So Harry dances. He dances to honour that time when they were happy. He closes his eyes as he dances and he sees Jules. Standing nearby, watching him. She's getting harder to see as the years go on but she's there, she's watching him dance. Harry's heart beats faster and he doesn't want to stop. Doesn't want to open his eyes. So he dances on in the rain. Not really knowing where he is or where he's going. Dances on and on because once his eyes are open and his feet stop moving, Jules will be gone.

Harry doesn't want to stop but Harry, of course, has to stop. It's not the cold or the wet that stop him, Harry is used to that, it's his lungs. His lungs that are used to slow plodding can't take the more rigorous action of dancing and they force him to rest. Once he stops dancing some sense returns and he moves to shelter from the rain before he is soaked to the skin.

It's hunger that Harry feels next and as he watches the rain clear he begins to think about where he is going to get some food. It's too early for restaurants and there aren't enough people about for begging. Harry decides to head for the Cross. He walks there, his stomach complaining all the way. The wet and cold sink into his shoes and up between his toes. It's worse to be cold and hungry but the walking warms him a little and then the hunger doesn't feel so bad. He could have caught the train. Could have slipped between the gates, fallen damp onto a seat for the short ride. He would have been rested then, maybe dried off a bit too. But the walking switches his focus, stops him thinking like he's been thinking. Stops him thinking about Jules.

As he walks he first thinks about the wet and the cold and the pain of the walk. Then he thinks about food. He sees the Cross covered with food, every corner a smiling face and an offer of food. He sees soft bread rolls and meat. Big, juicy lumps of meat. And potatoes. He sees his mum's Sunday roast all laid out on the table with knives and forks and cloth napkins. He sees the shining white jug filled with thick, dark gravy. And then he smells it, smells it as the roast comes out of the oven, as his mum carves it up and passes it out. First to his older brother, then his sister, then him. He sees his mum standing there, sweating a bit from the heat of the oven and the heat of the day, as she struggles with the knife that always looks too big for her hands. And then he laughs because his mum, the kitchen table, that gravy jug, they just don't look right in the Cross.

Sometimes Harry thinks about going back and seeing his mum. He wonders whether she'd cook him a roast. He reckons she would. He reckons she would sit opposite him and watch him eat, piling seconds and thirds onto his plate. It's a thought that almost makes him go. Almost. He reckons he could find the way. Then he remembers she's not there any more.

The last hill is a tough one. Harry is wheezing and puffing by the time he makes it up there. But once he enters the Cross he can smell the food in the air. He can practically taste it and he begins to forget all about that last bloody hill.

There was probably a time when Harry wouldn't eat out of a bin. Would never touch something that had been half eaten by someone else. That had the fingerprints and saliva of a stranger on it. But that time has well passed for Harry and though he tries to be careful, he's not afraid of putting his hand into a bin and pulling out a decent looking hamburger that's still half there.

He doesn't notice the people looking at him. Remains unaware of the children pointing or the adults shaking their heads, muttering to each other. He sees only the food and whatever other treasures may be lurking, hidden inside the metal of the bin.

When Harry has satisfied most of his hunger from the smorgasbord of the Kings Cross bins he finds himself a little spot out of the wind and away from the pedestrian traffic. And then he waits because there's no point coming all this way for just one meal. While he waits Harry feels the food in his stomach get heavier. His eyes start to droop. Harry curls himself into the tightest ball he can, resting his head on his knees. He allows himself a short doze and wakes with a start to find that it's dark.

At first he thinks he's slept too long, that he's missed the food he's hoping for and that he'll be walking home hungry again. It's hard for Harry to tell the time of day here. It's busy all the time. People pass in suits, in jeans, in outfits Harry doesn't have names for at any time of the day. It could be 6 p.m. or midnight. Harry has no idea as he walks away from his sheltered position. But when he gets to where he wants to go he sees that those people with their van are just setting up, just starting to serve and he hasn't missed a thing.

Harry takes his place in the queue and shuffles forward towards the food. It's not his mother's Sunday roast. He can see that from his place in the line. But it's hot and there's plenty of it and that's enough for Harry right now. Harry mumbles a thank you as he thinks he should when they hand him the steaming plate before he takes himself away from the crowds to eat in peace.

Harry eats fast. He wants to get all the warmth into his body as quickly as possible. He holds the plate close to his mouth and pushes the food in with the plastic fork. He's halfway through when the young bloke sits down beside him. Harry shifts a little, placing his back in the young bloke's face. Harry isn't interested in talking. He isn't even interested in listening. He's eating. The young bloke talks anyway.

He talks quickly and laughs a lot. Not real laughing but nervous, intermittent laughs like he doesn't know quite what else to do. Harry tries not to listen as the young bloke talks about good places to eat, good places to sleep. Harry has finished shovelling the food and is now licking his plate. He wipes his beard with his hand trying to catch any food that might be caught there. Then he puts down his plate and looks at the young bloke. He still looks fresh. Still a little clean on the edges. Bad skin and dirty clothes but still there's something clean about him.

The young bloke starts to ask Harry questions. Where does he sleep, does he eat at the Cross often? Harry just shakes his head. He doesn't need any more blokes down on his beach. He walks back to the van to return his plate to the people who are still busy, now packing and cleaning. Then Harry starts the long walk home, careful not to make eye contact with the young bloke as he leaves.

He walks slowly. The food is heavy and warm in his guts and he still feels tired from his short sleep. The air is cold on Harry's face and it pushes him forward, toward his bus shelter.

As he walks Harry tries not to think about the young bloke. He concentrates on the cars driving past him and remembers the joy of driving one. And then he sees the dog. It's lying in the middle of the road, its head on its paws. It looks like it's resting. Like it's waiting for the sound of its owner's feet, for the smell and rhythm of that one special person in its life.

Harry can see how it would jump up at the sound of that person, how its tail would wave and its tongue would fall out of its mouth in the joy of it all. Only the dog isn't moving. It's just lying in the middle of the road. Resting. Sleeping maybe.

Harry calls to it. He shouts "Dog!" because of course he doesn't know its name. But the dog doesn't hear him over the noise of the traffic and carries on in its peaceful pose as Harry calls and calls and the cars continue to roar around it. Harry sees that the cars don't slow down but how they seem to know the dog's there. They gently swerve around it. Like it's there every day and they are accustomed to having to drive around it.

Harry doesn't like seeing the dog on the road like that. He waits for a break in the traffic, thinking he will be able to wake the dog up and get it off the road. But the cars are relentless and Harry finds all he can do is stand on the side of the road and watch the cars drive around the sleeping dog. After a while Harry can't stand it any more. He gives up and continues his walk home.

Harry's never owned a dog. Never even really wanted one. But Harry knows about the dangers of cars and the need for a rest. Harry's seen a person or two get hit by a car. And he knows how hard it is to get a good sleep in sometimes. So on the way home all Harry thinks about is that maybe the dog will wake up. Maybe the dog knows what it's doing and will get itself off the road. It's not until his bus shelter's in sight that he realises the dog was already dead.

The CD she leaves in his bus shelter is her first purchase with the money she's earnt from her new job. The first non-essential purchase. She surprises herself by buying it. It's not something she'd ever thought she'd do. She didn't think she was so generous. She buys a copy for herself too.

There is no time to think about the dog when Harry gets back to his shelter because he can feel that something's wrong. Harry sits in his shelter and tries to ignore the feeling. He can't see anything obvious so he tries to believe it's just the dog that's got him all mixed up. But there's something else. No stupid yellow flower and all his stuff is still there but something, something's moved a little, changed a little. All Harry wants to do is lie down and sleep. But he can't sleep when he knows something's wrong.

Harry's been beaten up twice in his life so far and he wouldn't be shy about admitting he's scared of it happening again. It's there in his mind all the time. The worry of it. Before Harry was beaten, really beaten, he used to think there'd be nothing to it. He'd get hit, it would hurt, he'd get over it and he'd stop being afraid. That's because there'd only been scuffles. Young blokes puffing up their chests and smacking heads. A bit of pushing and shoving. Sure his mum hit him. Hit him all the time. But that was nothing either. Nothing like a real beating. A real beating is one that takes you by surprise. It shocks the air out of you. A real beating happens when you least expect it. When you're asleep, when your back is turned. And once it happens it doesn't take the fear away.

So that's why Harry stays awake. Why he forces his eyes to stay open. If something's changed, if something's about to happen, he's going to be awake for it. This time he wants to see it coming.

The first time, Harry thinks he probably asked for the beating. He came for Harry in the night but Harry started it during the day. The second beating was nothing to do with anything. Thugs with nothing better to do. Harry tries not to think about that any more.

Harry lies in his bus shelter and prepares himself for his third. He thinks about how he might protect himself. How he could run or fight. And then he sees it. Stuck in a spot where normally kids like to stick their empty chip packets that Harry then removes and licks clean, enjoying the sting of the salt on his dry, cracked lips. It's just a little spot between the boards of the shelter and one of the supporting poles.

It shines a little in the street light, then disappears in the brightness of a passing car's headlights. Harry sits up and grabs it. It's cold and hard in his hand. Harry turns it this way and that. It's a CD. Harry knows that but he can't make out the cover. Nothing to be afraid of though. That's the most important thing. Holding that CD tight in his hand, opening the cover and feeling the smoothness of the CD inside, Harry knows it's nothing to be afraid of and the knowledge makes him sleepy.

He doesn't need to think about whether the CD was left for him. He's too tired to link the appearance of the CD with the appearance of that stupid little yellow flower that drove him to distraction.

Harry lies back down on his bench with the CD tucked under his arm for safekeeping and he sleeps. The warmth from his body warms the plastic of the CD. Harry holds that CD there in his armpit until morning, and in the morning it is like the CD has become a part of him.

Harry wakes up to the sound of her coming down the street. He hears the pram being pushed out in front. The roar of the traffic, steadily increasing since before first light, doesn't stir Harry but that gentle squeak of the pram has his eyes open and his body alert. She's walking fast today. Her steps get faster and faster as she moves down the hill. As she gets closer Harry hears the child. It sets up a wail as it gets pushed along. Harry keeps himself still, he holds his eyes shut, and she flies past him without a pause, the way she usually does.

The child in the pram continues its cry. It's like a siren, fading as they move to wherever they are going in such a hurry.

Harry waits until he can no longer hear the crying child, then he sits up. He reaches carefully to where the CD is held and pulls it out. Then he reads the cover. Beethoven's 3rd Symphony. *Erotica*. Harry imagines a couple of kids. How they'd done a break and enter and come to his bus shelter to sort through their haul while he was off filling his guts at the Cross. How they came to this one CD, shook their heads and stuffed it in that little gap 'cause they don't like classical music or they don't think they'll be able to sell it. He sees them pushing each other, laughing. High on their success. He sees them joking, rubbing their hands together and speculating on what their haul will bring them. He sees them walking away, forgetting all about the CD they have unknowingly left for him.

Harry stands and puts the CD in his pocket. He walks slowly to the mall and as he's walking he shouts at people and cars, "What's the time exactly?" A young woman, a passenger in a blue sedan, winds down the window and tells him it's nearly ten o'clock. Harry picks up his walking pace and makes it to the Junction slightly out of breath.

The Junction has nothing much to offer this morning. People are hurrying, just as Harry is. People are cold, just as Harry is. Harry wonders who among these people has a CD in their pockets, as Harry does. Harry does not ask them though, Harry has only one question. He asks all that pass him. "What's the time exactly?"

After the first answer of "Almost ten," which is nowhere near as exact as Harry requires, he finds out that it is five minutes past from an old bloke who looks like he's barely left his bed and maybe shouldn't have.

Then everyone walks around Harry. No one will come near him let alone answer his question, until finally a woman, not much more than a girl Harry thinks, who holds a snotty-nosed kid on her hip, tells him it's 10.24 and Harry thinks this day will be a fast day and wonders, like he has many times before, how some days the clock can stand still and other days it moves so fast that it doesn't seem to take a breath.

After the woman/girl with the snotty-nosed kid, people become more talkative but the time doesn't slow down. A young man tells Harry it's 10.27 and then a fat man in a suit says it's 10.29 and Harry looks down and feels like he can see the earth spinning under his feet.

A bloke dressed casual like he's going to the gym but carrying a briefcase tells Harry it's 10.33 and a neat looking woman with three pristine children piled into a pram tells him it's 10.35. After that Harry sits down for a bit. He puts his hand in his pocket to touch the CD lying there and he turns to the old bloke next to him to say, "What's the time exactly?" And the old bloke, who was just about to nod off, jerks his head awake and tells Harry his watch broke. Harry nods. He understands. Harry's watch broke once too.

Harry soon pulls himself from his seat and a couple of schoolgirls, neat and nervous in their school uniforms, tell him it's 10.48 and then everything goes quiet for a little while and Harry begins to pace because he can feel he's near the end. The man behind the counter at the photo shop tells Harry it's 10.54 and after a little more pacing a fat woman in a faded dress tells him it's 10.57. Finally a girl with a tiny stud in her nose that glints in the pale sun light around tells him it's 11.01.

And then it's over and Harry can take his CD to the beach and think about what to do next.

Charlie is at the beach when Harry arrives. He wants to show his CD to someone so Charlie becomes the chosen person seeing as there's no one else around. Harry wants someone to agree with him. Agree it was just kids leaving it there.

Charlie has his bags piled up around him looking every inch the tramp that he is. He moves to protect his bags as Harry approaches but relaxes when he recognises him. He knows Harry won't want anything he has in those bags. Harry sits himself down next to Charlie and gives himself a moment or two to get used to the particular smell that surrounds Charlie. It's hard to tell if it's Charlie or the bags but there certainly is a smell that makes breathing a challenge. Harry is distracted by the thought that maybe he smells as bad as Charlie only he's gotten used to his own smell and for a moment he forgets the CD and thinks about how he'd find out, what he'd do about it, whether he would care.

"Cold enough for you?" It's the best he can do given the smell in the air, the questions rolling about in his mind and the CD in his pocket.

"Don't you go talking about the weather to me."

Charlie hates talking about the weather. Harry forgets that on a regular basis.

"Went down the Cross last night."

"Yeah?"

"Got meself a feed."

"Any good?"

"It was hot."

"Yeah."

"So what do you make of this then?"

Harry pulls the CD out from his pocket to show it to Charlie. He waves it in front of Charlie's face, scared to release it from his fingers in case Charlie nabs it and pops it into one of his bags, never to be seen again.

"It's a CD."

"Yeah. Someone left it in me shelter."

"That's a nice shelter you got there Harry. A man could get comfortable in a shelter like that."

Charlie starts rummaging around in his bags. Harry begins to foolishly hope he'll pull out a CD player because the longer Harry looks at the CD case the more he wants to hear what it holds.

As he watches Charlie rummage he says, "Kids probably" in the hope that Charlie will agree.

There's no nod of agreement coming from Charlie. He's still looking through his bags. Harry sits there in silence waiting for him until there's a sound like success that emerges from Charlie's mouth and he turns to face Harry with these stupid big glasses on.

He leans over and takes the CD from Harry's hands. Harry had decided he wouldn't let Charlie hold the CD. He thought that meant he'd never see it again. But now he's so stunned by the look of Charlie in his stupid glasses that he lets him take it without a fight. Charlie squints at the cover.

"Beethoven," he says.

"Yeah."

"E-ro-i-ca."

Harry snatches it back and corrects him.

"*Erotica.*" Harry already has a firm image in his mind of the music. Something passionate, about love and sex.

"Maybe it was that girl left it there for you."

"What girl?"

"That one with the kid you're always on about."

"Why would she leave me a CD?"

"Don't know."

"I reckon it was just kids." Harry tries to say this with authority in his voice so Charlie will agree but Charlie isn't buying this story.

"Kids?"

"Yeah. Kids." Harry starts to feel nervous.

"I don't reckon it was kids. You could sell this you could. It's Beethoven."

"No one listens to this kind of music no more."

"Tell that to me mum."

"Your mum's dead."

"Yeah well, when she was alive it was all she'd listen to."

"But she ain't alive now."

"Nah."

"That's me point. No one listens to this stuff now."

Charlie goes quiet. His gaze shifts away from Harry. He's not thinking about the CD any more. He's thinking about his mum. About a different time. Harry sees he's losing him. He tries to bring him back to the problem at hand.

"So what do you reckon I should do?"

Charlie says, "Sell it," and when he says it Harry realises he's been thinking that too. He's been wondering what it's worth and what he could get with the money. He puts the CD back in his pocket and says, "Yeah," like that's the plan even though he's not sure that's what he's going to do.

The two men sit for a time staring at nothing in particular. Thinking their own thoughts. Harry begins to tire of thinking about the CD. Charlie eventually stands and rustles his bags around for a bit before he says, "Well, I better be off." Harry doesn't ask him where he's going. He just nods his head and watches as he fumbles around with his stuff and when he's gone Harry slips his hand into his coat to make sure the CD is still there.

Charlie's smell lingers after he's gone. It lingers around Harry and Harry finds he doesn't mind it so much now he's gotten used to it. Then the sea air slowly dissipates Charlie's smell and Harry feels restless. Too restless to sit.

So he walks. He walks all the way to the headland. Something he doesn't do very often. He looks out over the ocean with one hand in his pocket, on his CD. Once or twice Harry takes it from his pocket and thinks about hurling it into the water. Then he could watch it as it sunk to the bottom of the sea. He could do that because it's his. Harry raises the CD above his head to feel the weight of it. Then he puts it back in his pocket where it's safe and wonders what it might sound like if it were played.

After that first purchase she finds she can't stop buying. She restricts herself to symphonies and tries to stick to a budget. Each time she buys one she tells herself it's the last. She's not sure how long she's going to have the job. How long there will be money for CDs. But then she finds herself stopping at another music shop on the way home from work. She buys only from the list at the back of the book. Trusting the book over her own taste. She ignores the ghosts who search through the CDs in the store and hold up their own choices for her to buy. Not all of the suggested listening in the book is easy to find. It's like a treasure hunt. Which is why, even when she tells herself she's only having a look, if she finds one she ends up buying it. She can't leave treasure lying in the store.

It's dark by the time Harry starts to head back to his shelter. On the way he finds himself standing outside a pub. A pub he knows would serve someone like him. "Drinking," Harry tells himself, and the woman walking by, "is the death of you on the streets." He tells himself this and anyone else who will listen, like he told himself the day before and the day after he last drank. And then he walks in.

It's quiet in the pub and not as warm as Harry expects. The smell of beer is strong and it brings saliva to Harry's mouth as he thinks, "Maybe I'll just have one." The bartender is young and looks bored but relaxed enough for Harry to approach. Harry walks quickly to the bar and as he's walking he takes the CD from his pocket and slaps it on the bar in front of him, "Play this for me would you mate?" The bartender looks at Harry and then he picks up the CD to read the cover. He shakes his head. "Sorry mate, I can't play that shit in here." Harry feels ashamed for no reason he could name, as he nods his head and quickly retrieves his CD. He leaves the bar forgetting about that beer he thought he might have.

As Harry walks the hill to his shelter the CD feels heavy in his pocket. He thinks again about throwing it away. And then he thinks about the other options he might have to listen to it. He thinks about stealing a CD player. But Harry doesn't do that. He thinks about it. But he doesn't do it. Never had the nerve or the dexterity and he doesn't want to live with any more fear than he's already got. So Harry thinks about going to a music shop and getting them to play it. And then he looks up and across the road he sees the library. It's small and set back from the road like it's trying to hide but Harry sees it and he rushes across the road ignoring the honking cars. He takes the stairs two at a time and when he pushes the door he's panting for breath.

The library, of course, is closed. Harry does not feel discouraged by this. He sits for a moment with the back of his head leaning against the closed door and he feels a sense of relief because at least now he has a plan. And then he walks slowly back to his shelter and prepares himself for sleep knowing that tomorrow he will hear his CD.

On the way back to his shelter Harry stops to ask for a bit of food from the nice people at the Vietnamese. It's a bit early but they give him rice and a small bit of meat with the veg and sauce. They give him the disposable chopsticks and paper napkin. Like they always do. Usually he tries to give back the chopsticks. Today he just takes them and gets out of their way quick. He can see they are busy. That it cost them to serve him.

Harry's sleep is restless as it is most nights. His stomach is not full enough and the CD still weighs heavy in his pocket despite his plan. He is impatient for morning to come but the night drags on and on.

When Harry is woken by the squeak of pram wheels he feels he has only just fallen asleep and in the scheme of things this is almost true. Harry lies on his bench and thinks about staying there all day as he listens to the pram wheels and the clip clip of her heels. He thinks about how he could rest all day as he sneaks a peak at her outfit and makes up a story about her day. She's in blue. That means she's tired. Her hair's pulled back away from her face. The baby's been up most of the night. If Harry was there he'd have said, "You stay in bed Jules, I'll take the kid for his walk." If Harry had taken on the role of father that he knew he never could be, that is what he would have said. That is what he would have done. What he would have been. And Jules would have loved him for it as she gratefully closed her eyes and settled back into the pillows while he took care of everything.

Harry lies as long as he can. Then he gets up quick. Rips off the bandaid. Tries not to think about it. Once Harry is up and moving he is in a hurry. He does not look at the people who tell him the time any more than he looks at the people who ignore him. He only cares about the numbers as he asks, "What's the time exactly?" He doesn't look at the way their eyebrows move when they tell him. He doesn't notice what they are carrying in their hands. He looks only at the numbers coming out of their mouths.

10.02, 10.04, 10.07, 10.11, 10.15, 10.15.

Time stands still.

10.16.

Time crawls.

10.22, 10.24, 10.28, 10.36, 10.40, 10.43, 10.45, 10.45, 10.47, 10.48, 10.49, 10.53, 10.58, 11.00.

Harry sets off out of the Junction and down the hill. He holds his hand in his pocket, his fingers lightly tapping on the plastic of the CD cover. He doesn't think. Doesn't plan what he'll say, what he'll do. He just walks.

The library is empty when Harry pushes the door open. Just a woman behind the desk. She looks busy but she raises her head when she hears the door open and she smiles at Harry when her eyes meet his. This smile invites Harry to approach, CD in hand. He shows it to the woman, who looks smaller now that he is closer.

She looks at the CD and back at Harry and she is still smiling as she says, "Beethoven hey?" and Harry says, "Yeah," because he doesn't know what else to say. The woman says, "Would you like to listen to it?" and Harry says, "Yeah" again and that's all he has to do.

The woman comes out from behind the desk and walks to where there are a number of computers lined up neat on the cold-looking desks. She pushes a button on the closest one and it whirrs and beeps as she takes the CD gently from Harry. Harry watches as the CD disappears into the computer and he hopes he will be able to retrieve it again. The woman, the librarian Harry is now prepared to call her, hands him a set of headphones and points to where they plug in. She shows him where the play button is and how to adjust the volume. Then she walks away. Returns to her desk and carries on with her work.

Harry sits down in front of the computer and slips the headphones over his ears. They feel soft and warm on his head. At first he hears only clicking and he begins to think this has all been for nothing. The CD holds nothing. But then he hears the music. It takes him by surprise. It's a good surprise. Harry turns up the volume and he allows his eyes to close. He finds he is not in the library any more. It's not winter, it's not anything. And Harry is nowhere. There's just music, as loud as it can go, filling all of the spaces in his body.

Harry keeps his eyes closed a long time. He hears a small noise outside of the music, feels movement by his side, so he opens his eyes and sees there is a cup in front of him. The cup is warm. Harry looks to the librarian and sees she too has a cup that she sips from so Harry takes his cup in his hands and enjoys the warmth that it gives him.

The cup holds soup. Harry sips it slowly while the music plays in his head and he wonders how long he'll be allowed to stay in the library. The soup is a cold empty cup when the music finally finishes and no one has disturbed Harry. No one has gone anywhere near him. Better yet, no one has asked him to leave. So Harry presses play again and listens to what is starting to sound familiar.

Harry doesn't find anything particularly erotic about the music but as it plays he tries to picture olden days people, locked in a passionate embrace. Mostly he sits there listening with a clear mind. He lets the music think for him.

The CD ends a second time and still no one has thrown him from the library. Harry decides to leave because if he leaves now then perhaps he can come back tomorrow.

With the music gone Harry begins to feel empty. The library is still and silent. Harry struggles with the computer, pushing every button he can see until finally the CD is returned to him.

Harry walks to the desk where the librarian sits immersed in her work. He hands her the headphones and says, "Thanks," in a voice not much above a whisper. The librarian smiles at Harry. She says, "Any time," in a voice that sounds so loud to Harry he almost jumps. But Harry understands what she has said. She has said that he can come back. He can come back any time. So Harry says, "See you," at what he hopes is a normal volume and the librarian smiles again before Harry turns and walks out onto the street.

The day outside startles Harry. At first he just stands blinking in the dull grey light before he remembers who he is and where he is and then he heads to the beach to scrounge for food and have a chat with the gulls.

Tonight, as she stands with her bag in her hand, readying herself to leave, telling herself not to go past that music shop on her way home, her attention is caught by the sight of a student. He's standing at her door, looking in. He's tall and slim with dark hair, not too long, not too short. She looks around the room to see what he is looking at, what he could want. No student has approached her before. The whole time she's been working there. It's like a rule that no one needed to explain. She looks at the ghosts, standing silently around her, ready for the trip home and wonders if he can see them too.

When she looks back he is still standing there, still looking. She looks at the shape of his hands. Musician's hands. Even from the distance she stands she can tell they're musician's hands. He looks European, kind of Italian but perhaps something else. Maybe something Slavic. She imagines a charming accent. An accent that places weight onto words and forces him to be creative with his limited knowledge of the English language.

It feels like a long time, the two of them standing, staring at each other. She looks down at her bag, at the papers around the room. She shrugs a little shrug with her shoulders and raises her eyebrows to him. Maybe he can't speak English. Maybe there's something he wants but doesn't know how to put it in words.

He smiles at her shrug and raised eyebrows. He smiles and in that moment she finds him beautiful. He opens his mouth but before any words come out Deanne pushes past him and into the room. She speaks quickly, firing off information about the next day. Deanne does not notice the student she's pushed past. The student still standing there.

As she's trying to concentrate on what Deanne is saying to her, she watches him walk away. At least he smiled. A smile is something. She really wanted to hear him speak. It's like he knew she was waiting to hear his voice and chose not to reveal it. She wonders again if perhaps he speaks no English. This could explain the long silence, the pause.

Thoughts of the silent student keep her occupied on the way home. She imagines scenarios that could have been. Ones where he speaks, where he sweeps her off her feet. Where they dance together into a future of love and happiness, music and good deeds for homeless people. These thoughts carry on as she makes her way onto the bus. They carry her to the Junction where she gets off the bus to do her weekly shop.

As she wanders the fluorescent corridors of the supermarket with all the other people who do their shopping on their way home from work, her mind starts to become filled with the practicalities of what she will eat for the coming week and the attractive student, probable musician, slips a little from the forefront. Her ghosts play among the aisles, marvelling at all the food available for purchase.

She is still careful with her spending around food. Still cautious as she fills her trolley with just enough. She still keeps a running total in her head, her recent extravagance with CDs hasn't extended itself to food.

She starts to think about the homeless man, about how much is enough for him to get by. She imagines herself inviting him to dinner. Perhaps if she got to know him the task of writing a symphony for him would become easier.

She thinks about what he may like to eat. When she first arrived in Sydney she offered half of her sandwich to a homeless man. She was sitting at the fountain in Kings Cross. The man came up to her and asked her for money. He said he was hungry. She was mid-bite through a large sandwich. So she offered the other half to him. The man said he didn't want it. Said he didn't like it. She can't remember what it was. Salad perhaps. She had to shrug. At the time it was all she had. She decides to buy a can of tuna. Maybe she'll make something for him with it. Something hot and healthy.

When she wakes in the morning she finds her courage has deserted her. It feels impossible to invite him to dinner. To even presume to cook for him. She can't think what she would say, how she would act. She doesn't want to offend him and she doesn't want to appear stupid. So she stays in her bed that extra half hour she thought she'd use to cook and she reads about Wagner, Verdi and Brahms until it's time to go to work and on her way she decides she will visit the homeless man in his shelter on Saturday. She'll visit and if he isn't there she'll leave the can of tuna in his shelter for him.

At work she finds herself standing at the doorway of one of the little piano rooms. The room is empty. In fact, the whole place is quiet. She must have arrived earlier than she thought. She looks up and down the hallway. Listens for the sound of students or staff, for footsteps and conversation. It's still quiet.

The ghosts push her from behind, force her forward. She steps into the room. Runs her hand along the piano. Not the keys but the wood. She runs her hands along the wood of the piano like it is precious, priceless. The piano is not priceless. It's a little scratched, a little unkempt but she's heard the sounds that these pianos make. The muffled sounds coming through the doors as students sit to practise. She's heard those sounds and she knows that these scratched unkempt pianos have the potential to be magic.

She stares at the piano and thinks about defeat. Is it time to accept defeat? It's been weeks now and all she has is a jumble of information in her head about dead composers, six CDs and a bunch of strange silent ghosts following her. She has a job, a job she quite likes but has no idea how long it will last and she has no idea how to write a symphony. And she has access to a whole lot of pianos she's too afraid to touch.

She sits down to face the piano keys. Today is not the day to accept defeat. She feels the ghosts gather silently behind her. She feels them holding their breath. They are waiting for her first note. Expecting genius. She tries to remember what it felt like when she saw the book sitting on the shelf, how eagerly she reached for it. She tells herself this is the same, all she has to do is reach out.

She brings her right hand forward and places it on the keys. They are smooth but not cold. She expected them to be cold. She places her thumb on middle C and lets her other fingers fall beside it. She presses her thumb down. The note is strong and it scares her. She looks around to see if the noise has alerted anyone but the place is still quiet. Even the ghosts are still. She reaches her arm out and shuts the door. She thinks, even if someone walks by, they will just think she is a student. That she is practising. If someone walks in and asks for the room. She'll just calmly stand up, smile, and leave.

Her mind flicks back to a book she used to own. A book of scales. At the time she barely opened it, hated using it. Now she thinks it could be useful.

She takes a breath in and plays the C scale. Just with her right hand. It comes easily and feels almost natural. She brings her left hand to the keys and tries a lower C scale. It's not so easy but it is still within her ability. She tries with both hands together. It's a little bumpy, a little uneven, but it's there. She can do it. Her fingers have remembered. She forgets the ghosts watching her and concentrates on her fingers, on the keys. She listens to the C scale as it flows from her fingers. She plays it again and again, her fingers running up and down the keys. Thoughts of defeat slip away. Anything is possible. She launches into the beginning of *Für Elise*.

It's dreadful. She stumbles, she forgets, she goes back to the beginning again only to stumble and forget some more. Beethoven crouches beside her in agony at hearing his work so clumsily played. She removes her fingers from the keys and puts her hands in her lap. She closes her eyes, breathes deeply, counts to three. Then she goes back to the C scale.

Just once more she tells herself. Just once more. When she is finally able to tear herself away, she sneaks back out of the room, heart thumping, sure any minute she'll be caught, questioned and banished. But somehow she isn't. Somehow it's okay just to walk out of the room and into her work.

Harry's days become routine. He wakes to the clip and squeak of heel and pram and then he gets his clock watching done. With business out of the way, he rushes to the library and bursts through its doors, CD in hand. After his first day Harry expected he would always find the library empty. Unfortunately for Harry this has not proven to be true. On the second day there are a group of school children whose chatter is momentarily halted by the somewhat dramatic arrival of Harry, bursting through the door, coat and hair flying, CD clenched tightly in his hand, tripping on the last step and falling, catching himself and falling again in a dishevelled heap on the carpet. On subsequent days there are pensioners, university students, mothers with children. But on every day there is the librarian, who always smiles when she sees Harry. Who always hands him a pair of headphones. Who always helps him to set up the computer until Friday when Harry proudly shows her he can do it himself.

Each day while Harry closes his eyes to let the music fill the empty spaces in his body a cup of soup is deposited in front of him. The soup doesn't fill him up. Hardly makes a dent in the pit that is his stomach. But it does warm him and it becomes intrinsically linked with the joy of the music.

On Friday, after Harry has proved he can operate a computer on his own and opened his eyes and drunk his soup, he gets very brave. He sees that there is only the librarian and himself and so he removes his headphones from the computer and lets the sound of Beethoven fill the library. The librarian lifts her head, at first shocked by the noise but when she sees Harry sitting at the computer, the end of the headphones in his hand and his eyes watching her, she laughs and shakes her head a little but doesn't stop him. Not until an elderly man pushes his way through the doors. Then she looks at Harry and Harry tries as quick as he can to push the headphones back into the socket. The library goes quiet and the librarian and Harry exchange a guilty look, like lovers caught in the act, thinks Harry.

Harry isn't sure he'll go to the library on Saturday. He thinks about everything else he could do. And then he goes. He knows she won't be there. She didn't say anything on Friday but he knows she won't be there. Harry walks in and tries to act as comfortable as he felt on Friday. He tries to ask for headphones like he's been doing it all week but actually he's never had to ask for headphones. The librarian has always had them ready. The man at the desk isn't rude. But he isn't nice either. There is no steaming cup of soup on Saturday and somehow the music is not as filling either.

Harry tries to concentrate hard on the notes. He tries to hold them in his head. But he can only listen once this day. Even though he hasn't got the notes right in his head, he can only listen once. Harry leaves the headphones at the desk. He walks out of the library hoping that the nice librarian will be back on Monday.

The rest of the day is spent sitting on the beach. He lets the sand fall through his fingers and listens for any notes that may still be in his head. Sometimes they are there in glimpses. Sometimes whole sequences. But by the end of the day the gulls with their squawking and carry on have drowned any of the music Harry managed to hold on to.

Harry remains at the beach until it is late and dark and then he slowly makes his way back to his shelter. He checks the bins for food on the way and finds enough to call it dinner.

Back at his shelter a can of tuna sits on the bench. Harry looks it over carefully because Harry knows you can never be too careful. But there doesn't seem to be anything wrong with the can. Except that it is not a can you can open with your hands. There is no handy ring pull on this can. This is one of those big cans of tuna that requires a can opener. And Harry does not have a can opener. He had one once. That was a bit of time ago now. He doesn't know what happened to it.

Harry does have a fork. He found it at the beach. Lying on the grass, shining in the sunlight of that day. Harry took it to the water and scrubbed it with sand and seawater. It's become one of his essential possessions. Harry feels a fork is superior to a knife or spoon. One tool that can do the job of many. But a fork cannot open a can of tuna.

Harry is not concerned about how he got the can of tuna. Not like he was with the flower or CD. Maybe he's getting used to finding things in his shelter. Or maybe it's because people often leave food for the homeless. Smiling people, like the librarian, who see them and want to help them. Christmas is especially a time people like to leave things. Harry has found cookies and cake in his shelter at Christmas time. Once there was even turkey. But at Christmas time it is warm and Harry knows it is nowhere near Christmas time.

Once there were these little kids. It was a while ago now. These little kids came up to Harry. Came out of nowhere. There were three of them and they couldn't have been more than seven or eight years old. They came up to Harry, right up to his shelter where Harry was sitting trying to get himself together for the day, and they handed him a package. Actually it was a towel wrapped up like a package. Harry took the towel package from them and they walked away. Didn't say anything at all. Just handed over the towel package and walked away.

If they had been a little older Harry would have suspected a practical joke and might not have looked inside the towel. But these children were young, they had looked straight at Harry with curious eyes. So Harry opened up the towel.

Inside there were a pair of shoes and socks, a can of food and soap. The can of food had a ring pull top. Harry didn't even think of it at the time but now, faced with the can of tuna he can't open, Harry understands that towel was packed by someone who knew their stuff.

Harry was pretty hungry the day those kids came up to him so he ate that can of food straight away with the same fork he carries today. Between mouthfuls he put on the shoes and socks. The shoes were a little tight but the socks were fantastic. Harry had forgotten what it felt like to wear new socks. That day he walked with a bounce in his step. That day and maybe a few others. The new sock feeling didn't last long but Harry enjoyed it while it was there.

Later that day, the day he was given the towel package, Harry ran into Jimmy. Jimmy isn't around the beach any more but back then he was and Harry considered him a good bloke. Jimmy was wearing new shoes too and he had the same story except Jimmy thought the kids were about ten. All through Sydney that day the homeless walked in new shoes with new socks. Some thought it was a school project. One reckoned they'd seen it on Oprah. Only Tony walked about in the same old shoes without socks. Somehow they had missed Tony.

Harry settles himself down for the night. He puts the can of tuna in his pocket next to the CD. Feeling it lying there makes Harry hungry again. Harry doesn't even like tuna that much. But he'd eat it now if he had a can opener.

Harry lies down and watches the cars drive past until his eyes start to feel heavy and fall closed. He thinks tomorrow he will go to find Charlie. Maybe Charlie has a can opener somewhere in those bags of his.

And that's how Harry goes to sleep. Thinking of Charlie and can openers and tuna falling down his throat. And it is not until morning that he remembers to be grateful he didn't lie awake all night hoping it was Jules who left the tuna.

And then it is Sunday. She lies in bed and thinks about the C scale. Her fingers crave the feel of the keys but there'll be no piano playing today. She sits up to practise on her pillow. Her fingers dance up and down the fabric. In her head she hears the notes.

She tries to remember back to the days of her music lessons. She wants to play the next scale. She remembers it had a sharp, and the next scale had two sharps but she doesn't remember which notes were the sharp ones. Perhaps if the piano were in front of her she could work it out by sound. Trial and error. Perhaps it is time for another book. She lies back down and closes her eyes. She listens to herself play the C scale, up and down, octave after octave, note after note.

But she cannot lie in bed all day, surrounded by the ghosts urging her to do something, be something. So she gets up, gets dressed and heads to the beach where she can sit and watch the pedestrian traffic pass by to the soundtrack of the surf. The beach is the one place the ghosts won't follow her. The one place she now gets to be truly alone.

It's not a busy day at the beach. A few keen surfers are out on their boards although there is little for them to catch. A bus arrives to unload tourists but only a few of them venture away from it, towards where she sits. Even fewer make it onto the sand and towards the water.

Winter is a time for the locals at Bondi and it's when she likes it best. Despite the wind and the rain and the cold, it's the time the beach belongs to those who live there. She loves to sit and watch, because there are always people, no matter what the weather, walking the prom, admiring the view, stopping to re-tie a shoelace.

She starts to think about her extras fund. Despite her extravagant spending on CDs, there's still money in her extras fund. She wants a portable CD player. One she can slip into her pocket. One with headphones. Then she could carry music with her, listen to her CDs anywhere she goes.

As she is trying to work out whether there is a store she can go to at the beach or whether she will need to go to the Junction, she feels a gentle tap on her shoulder. She turns to see Mark standing beside her. There's an awkward moment where he's standing and she's sitting and they're both waiting for the other. It's a power struggle between brother and sister. One they have played for as long as she can remember. One she never wins. As much as she hopes he'll sit, come down to her, she knows she has to stand. She stands and brushes herself off a little. Says hello.

Mark is with a girl he introduces but she quickly forgets the name in her effort to work out if it's the same girl he was with the day he helped her with the CV. She tells him about her job and tries not to sound too enthusiastic. He says, "You never told me, why music?" and she says, "Didn't I?" and tries to think of a way to change the subject. She can't, so she says, "I guess it's something I've always been interested in," and it's only when she says it that she realises it's true.

There is a pause in the conversation. Mark's companion looks bored and focuses on the ocean instead of the stilted conversation. Mark says, "You know Mum and Dad are talking about coming to visit," and she says, "Yeah, I wonder where they'd stay?" and he says, "Not with me!" and they laugh a little at the idea of living with their parents again even if it were just for a few nights. The girlfriend, because she has to assume it is a girlfriend, speaks up at this point to say that they really have to get going so goodbyes are said and they leave. She stands a moment watching them go, wishing he had suggested the girlfriend leave without him so that he could spend more time talking. Perhaps they would have talked for a while, really talked, about growing up or missing home or settling into the big new city. But instead she is left standing on her own wondering whether to sit again or head to the Junction.

It is a bleak day the day the library is closed. After clock watching Harry heads to the beach to look for Charlie. But the beach is cold and grey and Charlie is nowhere to be seen. So Harry returns to his shelter where he spends most of the day tapping his CD against his can of tuna. In the early afternoon Harry wanders to the library and rattles the doors. Just to check. Then he looks in the bins out the front and finds the better half of a sandwich. Harry does not see this as a good omen. He just sees it as half a sandwich. He eats the sandwich and returns to his shelter where he lies in wait for Monday.

It's pretty late by the time she gets to the Junction but she manages to find a suitable store that's still open. The range of portable CD players isn't large but they are fairly cheap. Well within her budget. She chooses a CD player and then spends some time deciding on headphones.

She knows that there are hairs in your ears. Little tiny hairs, and when there's a loud noise or you go to a loud concert those hairs inside your ears get worn down and they never grow back. This is how you lose your hearing. So she stares at the headphones and she worries about the tiny hairs in her ears. The store attendant doesn't seem to know anything about hairs in your ears but he assures her in a bored kind of way that they are completely safe and will not damage her hearing. It's really up to her how loud she chooses to play the music. This seems a sensible thing to say so she chooses the small pair and some batteries so that the whole thing will work.

She has not bought a CD with her so she has to wait until she gets home before she can try the player out. She chooses Mozart Symphony No. 39 because he is the composer she finds most light-hearted and the book says to listen to symphonies 30 to 41. In the beginning she has the volume down low because she is still thinking about the tiny hairs in her ears but about halfway through the first movement she turns it up a little, then a little more, and a little more still until there is no room left in her head for anything but the music.

This is when she realises that she has not really been hearing the music. It's been playing and she's been enjoying it but she hasn't stopped before and just listened to an entire symphony. She hasn't ever allowed the music to fully absorb her attention. There were always dishes to do, clothes to put away. Now, with her new portable CD player and little earphones, she lies down on the floor of the flat and lets the music take her where it wants to go.

As the music plays she closes her eyes. She sees surfers in the ocean, waiting for that one great wave. She becomes a surfer in the ocean, confidently astride her board, feeling the gentle rock of the water beneath her, the warmth of the sun on her back and a cool breeze through her hair, waiting, waiting.

She stays on the floor until she is cold and stiff, Mozart lying beside her, the other ghosts miffed that they were not the chosen ones to be played from the strange new device. She listens to that same symphony over and over. She crawls to bed with the ear pieces still attached and she falls asleep to the sounds of Mozart and to the feeling that somehow today she has made progress in her effort to write a symphony. Without even writing a note.

Monday clock watching is quickly over and the librarian is there when he arrives. She has been waiting for him. The appearance of Harry has added something to the librarian's days. He gives her a renewed sense of purpose. She feels, in some way, she's helping. And she realises she has always wanted to help. She remembers that this is why she became a librarian. To help people. She's always meant to help in other ways too. To serve dinners at Christmas, to donate time and money, to buy *The Big Issue* on a regular basis. She has always wanted to help. And here she is. Feeding, assisting a homeless man. There is a little bit of pride in her day that wasn't there before the appearance of the homeless man.

When Harry hears the music it is so familiar he can't believe he was unable to recall it. He listens straight through, twice. In between he sips on the cup of soup. At the end of the music Harry gets ready to leave. This is normally when Harry leaves. He listens twice and then he leaves. But today Harry pauses. It all feels so good sitting in the library, listening to music and sipping soup in a cup. Harry takes the CD slowly back out of its case. He slips it back into the machine. One more he tells himself, just one more, and he looks over at the librarian to see if she will disapprove. The librarian appears not to notice so Harry listens again. And again.

Harry spends the entire day sitting in the library. He dozes on his chair as the music plays in his ears. He eats half a sandwich that the librarian places in front of him and in the afternoon has another cup of soup. He loses count. It doesn't matter. It is a day of Beethoven. A celebration that the weekend is over.

At the end of the day the librarian gently touches him on the shoulder and he understands that it is time to leave. She locks the door after him, staying inside to finish her day alone. Harry stands for a moment on the steps, adjusting his eyes and body to the outside world. Then he makes his way back to his bus shelter where he sits watching the traffic and listening to the Beethoven that has remained in his head.

THIRD

When Harry opens his eyes and looks at the sky he sees blue. Cold, clear, clean blue. The blue tells Harry that winter will end. One day, winter will end, and Harry's day starts to feel promising. The pram passes quickly and Harry finds himself lying longer than usual on his bench admiring the colour of the sky. But when he throws back his blankets and greets the day he finds it's still winter.

Harry regrets leaving the warmth of his blankets as he stands in a small patch of sun, his arms spread wide trying to capture the warmth into his body. He stands there in the sun, its weak heat barely able to be felt on his skin, and he starts to think about coffee.

Harry tidies his blankets and checks his pockets, feeling the weight of the can of tuna against the lightness of the CD. He heads to the Junction. The sun has brought people from their houses. They have looked out their window and seen the bright blue sky and stepped out of their houses to enjoy it. Some have dressed badly, mistaking, as Harry did, the brightness of the sky for warmth.

As he walks to the Junction, Harry feels generous. Somehow he has given this day to the people who stand on the street and point their faces to the sky, believing the day to be wonderful. Harry decides he will not ruin the day for these people. He will not tell them that tomorrow the rain will fall and the wind will howl. He will let them enjoy this bright winter day and he will have a coffee.

Harry chooses a café set in from the mall. It's not too crowded. Most of the regulars have chosen to stay in the sunshine. There's a young man behind the counter operating a machine that hisses and steams. The young man sees Harry come in and raises his eyebrows at him. It's not an eyebrow raise of disgust or even of questioning what Harry is doing there. It's an eyebrow raise that says, "You're next. What do you want?"

So Harry says, "Couldn't spare a cup of coffee could you mate?" and the young man doesn't even blink or think, he just shrugs and says, "What kind?"

Harry doesn't know kinds of coffee. He only knows black or white. One sugar or two. He's heard of course. Heard of cappuccinos and lattes and other such things but he doesn't really know them so he shrugs back and says, "Whatever," and the young man nods and turns his attention to the machine that spits back at him. Harry's eyes wander around the café until they settle on the food on the counter. There's cream buns. Large cream buns. Harry can't take his eyes off those cream buns.

The young bloke puts a steaming cup in front of Harry and Harry takes it in both hands. With the cup safe in his hands, Harry pushes his luck. "Couldn't spare me a bun as well, could you?" The young bloke follows Harry's gaze to the cream buns. He reaches in with a pair of tongs and shoves one into a paper bag. Then he hands the bag to Harry. Harry says, "Thanks mate," and the young bloke nods to show he's heard but he's already moving on, his eyes seeking out the next customer, his eyebrows raised in their question.

The coffee is hot and milky and sweet. It feels so good in Harry's hands that for a long while he's happy just to hold it. He moves to a spot in the mall where the sun shines strong and he stands with his back to the sun and his hands wrapped around his coffee. The sun warms Harry's back, the heat of the coffee warms up Harry's arms. Harry thinks about the cream bun shoved into his pocket and he thinks maybe those people standing in the sunshine were right. Maybe it is a wonderful day.

Harry drinks his coffee slowly. He feels its warmth seep down into his body and a small amount of sweat breaks out on his forehead. Harry remembers other days when drinking coffee was a part of the morning. A part of the afternoon and sometimes a part of the night. When Jules or his mum would offer to make a coffee for him. And once in a while when he would do the same for them. It wasn't coffee like this though. It was coffee from a can. Good enough but nothing like this.

By the time Harry reaches the end of the coffee he's remembering something else about what drinking coffee does to a person and he starts moving quickly to the train station and into the toilets where he sits down and feels the shit rush out of him. Harry sits for a while after it's all over, to make sure it really is all over and when he emerges it's time for clock watching.

People don't like to be spoken to in public toilets. Harry knows this. Harry doesn't much like being spoken to in public toilets either but clock watching is different and Harry needs to know so Harry asks them. He says, "Can you tell me what the time is exactly?" and the men who look like they'd rather be anywhere else than where they are right now, check to see if they've got any way to get away from Harry and when they see they haven't they tell Harry it's 9.58, 10.00, 10.03.

Harry gets them on the way in and then he gets them on the way out. 10.05, 10.07, 10.08. And that's how Harry knows the bloke in the suit took three minutes and the bloke in the painter's overalls took one.

Harry gets tired of the stink in the public toilet. He leaves and finds a man with a large backpack on. Harry says, "Can you tell me what the time is exactly?" and the man searches around for his wrist and then his watch and tells Harry in a thick accent that it's 10.11.

Harry leaves the train station for the sunshine outside and shouts to a busker on the way "Can you tell me what the time is exactly?" but the busker just smiles and waves and starts playing his guitar so Harry asks a woman, an old woman, maybe a woman his mum's age and she tells him it's 10.16.

After that Harry starts to pace. Maybe it's the caffeine running through him. There aren't many people willing to tell him the time as he paces. One bloke moves so fast past him Harry never sees his face. He tells him the time though. Shouts it over his shoulder. 10.34, 10.34. Another stops and politely looks at his watch before muttering about it being broken and standing there fiddling and twitching and taking so long that Harry walks away. He finds a young woman sitting in the sun who tells him it's 10.47 and Harry gently feels the cream bun in his pocket and thinks, nearly, nearly.

Harry paces again until he finds a man in a suit who looks at his phone and tells him it's 11 o'clock and Harry says, "Thank you very much," and the man looks embarrassed because in truth he hasn't done that much but Harry smiles at him like he's done something wonderful and then he goes back to the spot he found in the morning and lets the sun settle on his back before he gets the bun out to have a look.

The bun really is large, even in Harry's hands. It's soft and powdery as Harry bites gently into it, careful not to eat too much too quick. Careful not to rush and drop and waste. The cream and jam make a mess of his hands and Harry licks his fingers because they have just been washed and because he does not want to miss any of the sticky sweetness. He eats the bun in small careful bites until there is only enough for one more bite. He pops this last bit into his mouth and holds it as long as he can before he chews and swallows. With the bun gone Harry shakes the icing sugar left in the bag into his mouth and feels satisfied with his morning.

There are students everywhere again when she arrives at work on Monday. On the bus she had imagined rushing straight in, straight to the piano, hardly stopping to take a breath before she launched into a few C scales as a warm-up to the exploration of which scale may be next. Now she can't play. Can't find that next scale. She still wants to buy a scale book but she has no idea where to look.

She makes her way to the room she is working in to find Deanne waiting for her. Deanne has some instructions for her, answers some questions and settles in for a chat. Some days Deanne rushes, rushes past, rushes in, rushes out. Some days she has time to stop. Time to talk. Some days she actively looks for a conversation.

She doesn't always know what to say to Deanne. There isn't often a lot to say about her life inside or outside of work. She can't tell Deanne about playing scales or writing symphonies or even about the homeless man. She tells her about the beach, about living in Bondi. Sometimes she makes up social events, a movie with a girlfriend or dinner at her brother's. Deanne talks about her kids. She complains about her husband and sometimes about work or the students who drive her crazy with questions.

She can't tell what makes it a chatting day or not but she enjoys the conversations when they happen and always feels a little disappointed when Deanne sighs and says, "Well I better get on with it," as she heads to the door. This time she stops her.

"Deanne?"

Deanne turns around. Looks carefully at her. "Yeah?"

"Where do you buy a book of scales?"

"Scales?"

"Yeah, you know, for playing the piano?"

"The piano?"

"Yeah. Not here. At home." She says it quickly in case Deanne becomes disapproving. In case she realises that she is thinking of playing the school's pianos. "I thought I might start playing again."

"And you want to start with scales?"

"Yeah."

Deanne smiles at her. "No idea." She starts to feel defeated. She's at a music school and she still can't find out what she needs to know. "But I'll find out for you." She smiles at Deanne, grateful for her kindness, her willingness to help without questions.

"Thanks."

Her day passes quickly. She works as hard as she can, losing focus only when she hears footsteps passing the room she's in. Any footsteps cause her to look up. She's hoping for Deanne to appear telling her where to buy music books. Hoping for the student from the other day to come back and finish whatever it was he came to say.

At the end of the day, after not seeing Deanne or the student, she seeks out Deanne to say goodbye. She is still hopeful but after saying goodbye and starting to turn away she thinks she will have to find another way to get the information she needs. She is at the door, turning into the hall when Deanne calls out, "Nearly forgot!" She turns to see what Deanne forgot, assuming it to be another piece of information about work the next day. But it isn't. Deanne has remembered to ask around and she has been told that the place to buy music books is in Glebe. A store that sells second-hand music books. Any book you could ever want. Deanne is pretty confident they sell books of scales. She tells her the shop stays open late most days. She doesn't need to hear any more. She thanks Deanne and rushes from the school, through Central and towards the buses that will take her to Glebe.

On the bus she places the headphones over her ears and the music that now fills her life, fills her mind. The ghosts join her on the bus. They seem to like new adventures. Particularly when it involves music.

The day is cold like all the others but the sky is clear and the sun is visible. There is no warmth to be felt from the sun but it is there. Just seeing it makes her feel a little more hopeful. Winter will end. She will learn how to play scales. She will learn how to write a symphony.

It doesn't take long to find the music shop. From the outside it looks like just another old shop. On the inside it looks like it's about to fall down. The walls are covered with posters that are starting to fade and peel away, taking some of the plaster with them. The floor is uneven and stacked with books and music scores. The stairs are narrow and look dangerous. It's like the whole shop is about to collapse in on itself.

For a while she is content just to browse. She looks at the books and music sheets stacked and packed into the space. She looks at the walls for any tell-tale signs of cracking and sinking. She breathes in the musty, dusty air and imagines it to be the smell of years of work from all the composers who wrote music before her.

She stumbles over a piece of carpet and finds herself in the learner's section where she discovers not one but many books, all displaying the various scales that must read like the alphabet to anyone who dares to call themselves a musician.

She chooses the cheapest book. Old habits die hard and she assures herself that they all look pretty much the same and checks that all the pages are intact just to make sure.

The ghosts are absorbed by the music shop. They love the variety of music held there. She thinks perhaps they will stay.

That she will lose them to this shop. She tries to call to them with her eyes, with actions that others would not notice. She's not ready for them to leave her.

Clutching her new book in her hands she walks back to the bus stop. Her ghosts follow behind. Some of them looking reluctantly back towards the shop they have just left.

She moves forward, thinking about courage and when it was that she lost hers. About whether she ever really had any. She thinks that if perhaps she did once have it, then she lost it only recently when she started to feel that her task was impossible because before then she was feeling pretty good about how everything was going. So if she lost her courage so recently, then, she reasons, there's nothing to stop her getting it back. It can't have gone too far in such a short time. The ghosts beside her nod. Like this is what they've been waiting for.

As Harry walks to the library he notices that people are still smiling. They're still happy with their day. Harry understands, he's feeling much the same way, but he can't help feeling they are all about to get disappointed.

There are a few people in the library today but Harry doesn't care about that. As long as the librarian is there behind the counter, ready to smile at him and hand over a pair of headphones. Harry heads to the computers with a growing feeling of satisfaction because he knows soon his head will be filled with music and when the music ends and he opens his eyes he will see a steaming cup of soup in front of him.

As Harry reaches for the CD in his pocket his fingers stray over the can of tuna but he lets it go and instead studies the CD cover as if there might be a clue there somewhere as to why he ended up with it. Harry opens the cover and examines the CD.

He doesn't understand how music comes out of there. He never understood how music came out of records either but at least they looked like they could hold something. The shiny round object in his hand doesn't look like it could hang onto anything.

Harry places it carefully into the computer and slips the padded headphones over his ears. When the music starts Harry stops thinking about where the CD came from. He stops thinking about how it is held on the disk and released as required. Harry lets the music take over his mind and body.

Harry listens to it twice like he always does. The second time he listens he sips his soup. It's a calmer listen that second time. The urgency is gone. The music can be a little quieter, Harry can allow his eyes to open and look around. He shifts in his seat. It's hard to keep still so long. It makes his arse ache.

When it is over, Harry sits a moment with his aching arse and ringing ears and then he slips the CD out and his headphones off. Harry returns his headphones to the librarian and heads for the door when he hears her voice. "We have others you know." Harry has to turn around to make sure she's talking to him and to see what she's talking about. She smiles when Harry turns and she points to another section of the library. Harry squints a little and sees other CDs, stacked like he's seen them in a CD shop. She says, "Maybe you'd like to listen to some other music one day," but Harry shakes his head. "I like this one," and the librarian smiles like that's okay and so Harry feels it is. And then Harry is out the door and on the way to the beach.

As Harry gets closer to the beach he feels the tuna in his pocket and he thinks about finding Charlie. But Charlie doesn't appear to be at the beach again today and Harry is pretty sure he isn't because Charlie is easy to spot. There isn't anyone else around who might have a can opener so Harry finds himself a spot on the grass like most of the others around him are doing and he lies back to admire the wonderful day.

Harry watches the clouds move gently across the sky. They move to the music still in his head and the music makes the clouds beautiful. Harry lies like that, watching the clouds move to the music in his head until he gets the feeling he's being watched.

Harry sits up and looks around. His first thought is maybe it's Charlie, maybe he's got a can opener and they can share the tuna. But the first thing Harry smells when he sits up is not Charlie's distinctive stench but an orange. There's a girl sitting next to Harry, just to the right of him, eating an orange. The girl is wearing a skirt and bra. Her shirt lies discarded next to her. This is something Harry's got used to seeing over the years.

Harry doesn't wonder any more about what kind of girl it is who will sit in a park in her bra. He used to. Used to stare and stare. Where Harry's from you don't show your bra. But the girls here, girls from other countries, they think it's all right. Today Harry stares, but he's not staring at the bra. It's the orange. It's been a long time since Harry had an orange.

The smell and sight of the orange makes Harry's mouth water. It makes him hungry and thirsty at the same time. The longing is unbearable. So he stops staring. He tries to stop smelling. Instead he looks at all the other people and there's plenty to look at today. There are people sitting on the beach and a few surfers in the water. There are dogs being walked or roaming around free with their owners somewhere behind.

The orange smell fades and when Harry looks back at the girl in the bra, she's gone and she's taken her orange with her. Harry prepares to lie back down again but he remembers that feeling that someone's staring at him so he looks around more carefully this time turning his head so quick that it cracks and hurts. It's while Harry is rubbing his neck that he sees Bloody Brian standing off to his left.

Harry turns back quickly hoping that Bloody Brian did not see his look, did not take recognition for invitation. Harry sits still. If he's still and quiet he won't be approached. Harry's nose starts to itch and his eyes start to water but he doesn't move. His muscles start to ache with the tension and it is all for no use anyway as Bloody Brian comes and plonks himself down. Even when Bloody Brian is sitting there, right next to Harry, he stays frozen. He has become trapped in his own stillness and is unsure whether he could move, even if he wanted to.

Bloody Brian shuffles around on his butt making himself nice and comfortable but Harry stays still. He says, "Hello Harry, how are you then?" and Harry tests his mouth to see whether it's capable of moving. It isn't. Bloody Brian carries on like Harry has answered. Like Harry is sitting there inviting conversation. He says, "Lovely day, isn't it?" and then he throws a warm bundle of paper into Harry's lap. The warmth of the bundle spreads through Harry and the stillness disappears. Harry holds the bundle to his chest and thinks he will have to pay for this. Somehow, Bloody Brian will make him pay for this.

Harry considers his options. He could throw the bundle back to Brian. Throw it back and walk away. But that bundle is warm and smells of grease and salt and Harry can feel inside that bundle there's a piece of fish nestled among a mountain of chips and it's hard for Harry to throw that away. So he stays. He rips a small hole at one end of the package and he draws out the chips, one at a time. Nice and slow.

Bloody Brian says, "Beer?' and he holds up a couple of cans of light beer. Harry looks at the beer. As far as Harry's concerned only poofs drink light beer. Harry didn't know Bloody Brian was a poof. He's about to say it. About to open his mouth and say "I didn't know you were a poof, Brian," but that would be talking and Harry's not ready to talk yet so he shakes his head and watches as Bloody Brian shrugs and opens one for himself. He takes a big long drink and then he sighs like it tasted really good and places the beer beside him so he can concentrate on his own paper package. Harry turns his attention back to the ocean and the feeling of warmth coming through his bundle so he doesn't regret that shake of his head.

As Harry eats, he watches Bloody Brian from the corner of his eye. He never turns his head but he watches. Waits. Bloody Brian spreads his legs out in front of him and places his package in the middle. He opens the package into one big square, food exposed for all to see. Harry snorts. Idiot. The gulls are quick to notice Bloody Brian's mistake. They hover as close as they dare, inching onto the paper in an attempt to steal a chip. Those on the outer start to crowd around Harry. They can see he has food too. But Harry does not share his food with gulls.

Bloody Brian eats quickly. He shoos the gulls with one hand while he shoves in chips with the other. He eats like a man in a hurry and before Harry's even halfway through Bloody Brian has finished and is back to his beer. He throws the crumbs at the gulls which causes a flurry of feathers and noise.

"Saw you coming out of the library."

Bloody Brian speaks after the noise of the gulls has dulled down. He doesn't look at Harry. Instead he looks around on the ground like maybe there's a spare chip. There isn't, but he sees his beer so he picks that up instead and finishes it off. Harry keeps eating. Nice and slow. He's found the fish now and Harry knows you have to be careful when you eat fish. So Harry chews nice and slow.

"What were you doing? If you don't mind me asking?"

Harry keeps chewing until there's nothing left in his mouth. Until he's chewing his tongue. He thinks about saying he does mind. But the truth is he doesn't so he shrugs and says, "Listening to music," and Bloody Brian says, "Music?" and he sounds very surprised so Harry says, "Don't suppose you have a can opener on you?" Because that's really what Harry's interested in. Bloody Brian gets distracted by the can opener question for a bit and pats down his pockets before shaking his head. Then he remembers that Harry's been in the library listening to music and he asks Harry what he's been listening to.

But Harry has returned to his fish and his mouth is full so he just keeps chewing and it's up to Bloody Brian to keep up the conversation.

"I like music. All kinds of music."

And Harry nods because Bloody Brian is looking at him and expecting some kind of response. Bloody Brian looks back at the ocean.

"Used to listen to it all the time. All the time."

There is another pause as Harry eats his chips and Bloody Brian contemplates opening the second beer.

"So what are you listening to?"

Harry reaches into his coat and tosses the CD to Bloody Brian. He tries to do it casually but actually he's scared. Scared to have the CD out of his reach. Bloody Brian takes the CD carefully, like he knows it's precious and looks at the cover. "Beethoven," he announces. And then, "*Eroica.*"

Harry takes the opportunity to snatch it back from Brian. He corrects Bloody Brian as he gets the CD safely back into his hands. "*Erotica.*"

Bloody Brian shakes his head. He leans over and points to the words on the CD cover. The words Harry has looked at a million times but never actually read. "E-R-O-I-C-A." Harry sees that Bloody Brian is right. He doesn't like it. He puts the CD safely back into his coat.

"Know what it means? *Eroica?*"

Harry shakes his head.

"Hero."

The new title has changed the music. It makes some sense to Harry, those passionate embraces he pictured, never felt quite right. He needs to hear it again. Would like to be in the library right now with the music in his ears and Bloody Brian out of his head.

"He starting writing it for Napoleon, but then he changed his mind. Called it Hero instead."

Bloody Brian's knowledge is annoying. Like he's trying to take something away from Harry. Make the music something that can't belong to Harry.

Bloody Brian runs his hands through his hair. It's a good amount of hair that Bloody Brian has, it makes him feel like he's sorting things out when he runs his hands through it. And some days he does sort it out. Some days he gets to bed and he thinks he's done okay. And then he wakes in the morning with the knowledge that there's so much more to do and he runs his hands through his substantial amount of hair and gets on with it.

Harry watches Bloody Brian's hands and his hair and then he thinks about his CD and whether it's going to be the same now the title's changed. He doesn't hear Bloody Brian talk about Beethoven and greatness and how it's a different world now and we've all got to get by as best we can. He doesn't hear Bloody Brian sigh and admit he's bloody tired.

The ocean picks up its roar a little as the tide starts to come in. Both men stare at the waves. There is a coolness coming off the water. A sense that the night is on its way even though it's only midway through the afternoon. Harry is thinking about his head. His head, his stomach, the great thirst that has suddenly overtaken him. He doesn't know how long it's been since Bloody Brian stopped talking but he feels it's time for him to say something. He'd like to stand up and walk away. Go look for something to drink. He'd like to not say anything. But he feels he owes something to Bloody Brian. It's the problem with people giving you food.

So Harry says, "It makes me feel alive." And it's only when Harry says it that Harry realised how little he thinks about being alive and how unimportant it has always seemed.

Bloody Brian looks surprised. Maybe surprised Harry has spoken. Maybe surprised at the depth of what Harry has said. That is, after he works out what it is that Harry has said, because Bloody Brian moved away from thinking about music and Beethoven a while ago. But after the surprise Bloody Brian nods his head and gives Harry a little smile. He says, "Yeah," and makes Harry feel he was right to speak.

Then Bloody Brian stands up and starts to make like he's going to leave. He brushes the bits of dirt and grass off his bum and shoves the unopened beer into his pocket. He starts to look all business and busy the way Harry is used to seeing him. As a goodbye he says to Harry, "I could get you others if you want. Other CDs to listen to." But Harry shakes his head. "I like this one." Harry doesn't think there's room in his life, in his head, for another CD. Bloody Brian shrugs fair enough and thanks Harry for the company and conversation. Harry snorts quietly to himself. He knows he should be thanking Bloody Brian for his full belly but it's not something he likes to say. So he says nothing. Turns his attention back to the ocean and the gulls and the people walking by and pretends not to even notice Bloody Brian walking away.

She tells herself there's nothing wrong with playing the C scale on a piano. Nothing to feel ashamed or embarrassed about, despite what some of the ghosts seem to indicate. She decides that if she gets another chance she will sneak into one of the piano rooms and play scales. She will do this any chance she gets. She will do this because she has courage. She decides to tell someone about the symphony she plans to write. This will make it real. This will mean she has to do it.

She ignores the fact that opportunities to sneak into those rooms are rare. Ignores the fact that she may put her job in jeopardy. She focuses on courage.

She practises telling someone about her symphony. Maybe Deanne. Deanne will ask her if she found the shop. If she found the book she was looking for and she'll say yes and thank her for the information. Then Deanne will say, "How are the scales going at home?" or maybe she'll talk about work or her kids. But if Deanne gets off subject she'll interrupt her or maybe just wait for her turn to speak and then she'll say, "I am preparing to write a symphony. A symphony for the homeless man I saw from the bus."

Maybe Deanne will tell her she can use the piano rooms. That she can book them like the students do. So long as she does her work, she can practise in her lunch break or when she's finished if it's something she really wants to do. Maybe Deanne knows a teacher who would be willing to help her.

But she doesn't see Deanne on this day when she is being courageous. She spends her day working through the shelves of music quietly on her own. She puts aside the ones she has questions about. Glances through the ones that catch her eye. She tries to read the music, tries to hear it as she reads.

Towards the end of the day someone walks into the room. She looks up, expecting to see Deanne and she sees that it is the student again. She smiles. She doesn't plan to smile, doesn't know why she smiles but she smiles. He smiles back. He looks even nicer when he smiles.

She moves slowly from the step ladder she is on, hoping that turning her back won't encourage him to disappear again. With her feet firmly on the ground she looks at him, wondering what to say. Wondering if she is about to just blurt out that she is writing a symphony. As she turns she hears him say, "I'm sorry to bother you." The voice is very Australian, no hint of Europe in it at all. She says, "You're not bothering me," and smiles again.

He says, "I'm looking for a piece of music. I wondered if you might have come across it." She says to him, "Are you a student here?" and he says, "Yes." She asks him what he is studying and he says, "Composition."

The surfers start to leave the water. One by one they swim to shore. When their feet hit the sand they start to run. Some stop to pick up a towel or some keys before they jog to their cars but others just run. They don't stop to pick up anything. Just run over the sand and up onto the prom. Over the prom and onto the grass. Then they keep running over the grass. Harry imagines them running across the road, down the street, until they get to their houses and there they keep running. Drop their boards and keep running till they get to the shower where they turn the water on full and strip off their wetsuits while they wait for the water to start steaming. After their shower, when they're warm and dry, they go to the kitchen and heat up a pie in the microwave. Eat it while they're still standing up. It will be the perfect end to a perfect afternoon.

Harry can see the sense in it. Can see that it would keep you warm all that running. But he can't be much bothered to do it himself. Probably wouldn't be able to make it up the hill. Not worth trying. It gets cold though, sitting on the grass. The sun goes down real quick in the winter. You forget how short the days can be.

When the cold has soaked through Harry's clothes and into his arse he gets up and drags himself away from the beach. Most are leaving now. Probably, Harry thinks, the cold has made it into everyone's arse and they've had enough. But as Harry's slowly getting up the hill he sees Charlie, sitting over in one of the shelters.

During the walk to where Charlie's sitting, Harry sticks his hand in his pocket and lets it seek out the can of tuna. Probably the tuna should be saved for a day when there's less food about but Harry would rather eat the tuna now than have to carry it around. Would rather eat it than have to think about it any more.

Harry sits down with Charlie and they do a quick swap of their day. Harry doesn't tell Charlie about Bloody Brian and the beer and chips. But he does tell him about the coffee and the cream bun. Charlie lays out the treasure he found that day for Harry to have a brief look at. Metal today. An old fork, the lid of a drink bottle and one earring with long dangling bits that Harry would laugh at if he didn't know better. Charlie quickly sweeps the pieces into his bags where they are secreted away. And Harry takes the opportunity to place his can of tuna on the table instead.

Charlie stares at the can. He hasn't eaten much that day, he's been thinking about metal. Shiny, shiny, metal. Here it is in front of him. Shiny metal with something to eat inside. He wants it. Wants it as much as he wants anything he sees on the ground that glints and gleams. He wants the tuna but he doesn't have a can opener. Had one once. Used to have one. Checks through his bags. Then checks through again. Must have one somewhere. But no, there's no can opener to be found.

The men sit silently together. One staring at the can of tuna, willing it to open. One staring at the sky, watching it change from blue to black. Poor Charlie is hungrier than he knew. The can of food sitting there is almost too much to bear. Harry doesn't see Charlie's frustration. He's not looking at the can of food. He's looking at the night arriving. Watching as the gulls prepare for the coming cold.

The gulls fluff out their feathers and huddle together. They cling together, sharing their warmth. Harry wonders if gulls sleep. If they ever close their eyes and go into a deep sleep where everything is forgotten. Or if they, like Harry, are always just dozing. Waiting for an expected yet surprising moment of danger or for a sudden windfall of food.

Harry feels tired sitting there with Charlie. His body aches for sleep and he starts to long for his bus shelter. It takes a while to move. Takes a while to muster the energy even just to reach his hand across and slide that can of tuna back into his pocket. Charlie follows the can with his eyes. Follows it the whole way across the table. It's only when he hears the clink of the can hitting the CD in Harry's pocket that he tears his eyes away.

The men don't say goodbye to each other. They don't wish each other a safe night, they never talk about it. There is nothing to say. So it is more of a nod, sigh and grunt as Harry gets himself to his feet and moves off towards the hill. Charlie is still thinking about the can of tuna. The can of tuna and more importantly, where he last saw a can opener. He doesn't think about the hardships of the night to come. Where will he sleep? What will he eat? He just thinks about can openers. He will think so long about can openers that he will decide it's too late to move. And then he will just build up his bags around him like a wall and a blanket and stay there.

It is not classical composition. It's modern. Short, sharp, modern songs. She is not disappointed. He tells her the music he is looking for but she has no recollection of it. She explains she hasn't finished the stocktake. That it might be here but she hasn't come across it yet. She tells him she's interested in classical music. That it's the classical music that catches her eye. But, she tells him, she'll look out for it now. She'll let him know if she finds it.

She confesses in this first conversation with the composition student that she is planning to write a symphony. He doesn't laugh at her. He gives her his phone number. Writes down his name. Denis. Not the name she would have expected, just like it's not the accent she imagined. She decides in this first conversation that she likes both the name and the accent despite this.

He says, "Call me if there's anything I can help you with." She takes his number and places it carefully in her pocket. She says, "Okay, I will," and she means it even though her heart is pounding and she's so scared of doing or saying something wrong that she thinks she might cry just from the sheer strain of it all.

Harry makes his way slowly up the hill. The winter is hard on those who live outdoors. Sometimes it comes early and it stays long and blows hard. Sometimes the weather stays warm and you can almost believe that it's not coming. But winter always comes and it's always hard. Harry concentrates on putting one foot in front of the other. He tries not to dwell on the length of winter or even on the length of the night ahead. Just keeps himself upright. Hands in his pockets. One foot in front of the other.

There are not many cars on the road as Harry walks. A few people here and there, all looking cold like they have been surprised by the speed that night has fallen. Some look tired, look as tired as Harry feels. And then there are others. Others who are dressed warmly and have energy in their step. People who are heading out for the night and who are prepared for all the night holds.

Harry continues to walk. One foot in front of the other. He keeps his head down and his hand on the can of tuna and CD although it doesn't stop them knocking together in his pocket. He concentrates on the sound they make as he walks. He starts to hear a rhythm, a beat. And before you know it Harry is hearing music in his head. The music makes him stride. It makes his steps large and energetic. Harry is a soldier coming back from war. A hero, just like Bloody Brian said. It no longer matters about the cold or the constant tiredness, or even that little edge of hunger that's coming back to haunt him. Only the music matters.

The music and Harry's striding step, one foot in front of the other all the way up the hill and home.

He's out of breath when he gets to his shelter. Out of breath and sweating under his winter clothes. He sits down on his bench, rests his head against the back wall and tries to breathe. His head is spinning a little and he finds he has to sit and wait a while before he can lie down.

After all that striding Harry sleeps more soundly than he normally does. For a short time there is a warmth in his guts and heat in his lungs and this allows him to fall asleep quickly and deeply.

Harry wakes in the morning to the sound of pram wheels and stepping feet. It's another sunny day. Harry can tell before he opens his eyes. He can tell by the sound of those feet before he's even felt the sun on his face. She walks like it's going to be wonderful day again.

She wears yellow today. Bright yellow. Harry has never seen her in yellow and he steals glances at her as he lies perfectly still on the bench. She looks cold and walks quickly. She has dressed as if it were already summer and Harry worries that she will spend the day regretting her choice. She hums to herself too. A hum that is too quiet to be for the child's benefit so can only be for hers.

The child in the pram has grown. Seems to grow each time. Today he looks happy. He is dressed for winter with a rug over his lap and eating some kind of biscuit that has turned into a soggy mess all over his face.

Harry lies still and watches them pass. He thinks again about where they might be going and wonders why he never sees them come back. Harry lies there until he can no longer hear her step, can no longer remember the sound of her humming and can no longer smell her perfume. Then he lies a little longer still in an attempt to avoid just a small part of the coming day.

Once Harry is up he starts to think about the coffee he had the day before. He remembers the smell and how it felt moving down into his guts. He forgets the shitting and the pain. He wants another one.

So he makes his way to the Junction and to the same café, hoping that the same bloke will be there with his slight smile and his nod. On his way people pass him and most of them smile like they did the day before thinking that this too will be a wonderful day. They ignore the cold wind that takes away any of the heat the sun has to offer. They tell themselves that winter is over. But Harry, he feels that cold wind and he sees that clouds are coming.

Still, he moves forward through the cold wind towards that coffee and when he gets there he finds the café crowded. The bloke from yesterday is there and he acknowledges Harry with his eyebrows just like he did the day before and Harry relaxes and feels he is about to be looked after.

But there is another bloke. An older, fatter bloke who does not have that same calm reassuring look. This bloke sees Harry and starts to shout. Harry doesn't understand why. He doesn't understand what the man is saying. But he does understand that the man is shouting at him.

Harry is still for a moment. Caught in the glare of the fat man's shouts. He becomes lost and unable to work out which way to turn. He looks to the young bloke for his reassuring nod but the young bloke simply shrugs and looks as helpless as Harry feels. So Harry blunders this way and that until he finds the door and is out onto the mall. And then he just stands still. He feels numb in the brightness of the sunlight and the coldness of the wind. He stands until the cold wind blows the shouting from his ears.

When there is stillness and quiet in Harry's head he starts to ask the time. He turns to the people who pass him and he says, "What's the time exactly?" At first no one answers. They are busy getting on with their day and Harry is muttering under his breath, still in a state of shock. He keeps asking, "What's the time exactly?" and people keep walking past him. He starts to speak a little louder. Tries to make the words clearer. And still they walk past him. But Harry keeps asking. He keeps asking until a small girl comes to tug at his coat. The girl is so small it's hard to believe she understands what time is. She tells Harry the time is 10.16 exactly and she tells him she knows that it is exactly this time because she rang up the clock on the telephone this morning and found out.

Harry watches the little girl as her mother comes to take her away from him and he feels a little safer in the knowledge that it's important to someone else to know what the time is exactly. And then he looks to the café and sees the fat man standing in his doorway, watching Harry, waiting to see his next move, and Harry is struck by stillness again. He stops seeing faces, stops hearing words. Everything blurs and at first he hears the fat man shouting again only he can't make out the words and then he realises that the fat man isn't shouting, the fat man is singing. He's singing Beethoven and it all begins to make some kind of sense.

So Harry continues with his question. He says, "What's the time exactly?" only now he's kind of shouting so that he can be heard over the fat man singing Beethoven. No one answers but Harry keeps shouting. Keeps shouting until his voice is hoarse. Keeps shouting until the fat man retreats into his café. Keeps shouting until an old man with watery eyes comes over and holds his arm and says, "It's 11.34 son." And then, and only then, does Harry stop shouting.

Harry turns his back on the Junction and walks towards the beach. He ends up at the library. He really did mean to go to the beach but habit seems to lead him up the library steps and before he really understands what he's doing he's sitting there with headphones on and music filling his head. A different librarian gives him the headphones without a smile but without a frown either. Harry shuts his eyes to the morning and lets the music take him away.

The music enters his body. His breathing slows. His head is heavy and his arms and legs feel like big soft mattresses. Harry feels safe as he falls asleep in the library and not at all embarrassed when he wakes up at the end of his symphony.

Later Harry finds himself at the beach. It's more crowded than the day deserves. Clouds now cover the sky. Every now and then the sun appears as a reminder of what warmth is only to disappear again to plunge everyone back into the cold misery of winter.

Charlie is sitting in the same shelter. Perhaps he never left. He waves to Harry. Waves something at Harry. But Harry isn't ready to talk to Charlie so he finds himself a spot on the damp grass and watches the gulls for a while.

There's a young man walking down on the prom. He looks a bit rough, a bit lost. He walks past Harry, looks at Harry. Harry looks quickly away. Harry knows his type, has seen his type. Maybe even was his type once, but Harry doesn't want to be talking to that type today.

Before, a long time before today, Harry would have these

young men coming to him every day. They would come and sit beside him. Always men, always young men. Always wanting to tell Harry their story.

Sometimes he could be kind. Could listen with some attention. Sometimes he would even give them a tentative pat on the shoulder. Sometimes he would tell them anything he thought would help. He'd tell them, "Stay away from booze, it's the death of you on the streets." He'd tell them to keep a close watch all the time. "Time gets slippery on the streets," he'd say.

Other times he would look away. Try not to hear what he was being told. Some days he would just stand up and walk away.

Now he doesn't want to know. Now he cannot be kind. So he takes the Charlie escape route. Rarely will a young man approach the two of them sitting there. Harry walks as fast as he can towards Charlie. He walks so fast up the hill he feels like he's running. And then he sits, panting, watching Charlie, neither of them speaking but Harry knowing that Charlie has something he needs to say. That he's just waiting for the right time.

Charlie doesn't need words. Charlie has something in his hand and he places it on the table between them with all the ceremony that the object deserves. Harry picks it up. It looks like a twisted old piece of metal but on closer inspection Harry sees that it's a can opener. Charlie is looking so pleased with himself that Harry decides not to say the can opener belongs in the rubbish bin and if they use it could well be the death of them both. He decides not to say anything but to instead give Charlie the silent ceremony he so obviously wants.

Harry reaches deep into his pocket and pulls out the can of tuna. He places the can and the opener onto the table and the two men sit a while and look at them. Then Charlie shoots Harry a quick look before he makes a grab for the can and the opener.

Harry is probably a good ten years younger than Charlie. He is also a lot faster. Harry's hands cover the can and the opener before Charlie's fingers reach them and Charlie retracts his fingers, puts them carefully into his pockets like a naughty child. Then he waits.

It's hard work getting that opener around the top of the can but eventually Harry and Charlie find themselves in front of an opened can of tuna. There's a lot of juice in the can and Harry wants to pour it out onto the grass but Charlie won't let him. Charlie declares that the juice is, "Good stuff," so the two men dig the tuna out around the juice and the rough metal edges the opener has left.

It doesn't take long before the tuna is gone. Charlie spends some time sticking his fork in and searching around for small bits of fish long after Harry has given up. Harry points to the left over juice and asks Charlie what he plans to do with it. Charlie says, "Drink it," and then he looks at Harry to see if Harry is going to lay claim to the juice. Harry says nothing. He wants no part in the tuna juice.

Charlie examines the can. He is not willing to risk his lips by drinking straight from those rough edges so he begins to rummage through his bags. The rustling and carry on with the bags starts to get to Harry and he thinks about leaving. But then the rustling stops and Charlie produces a beer glass. An old, scratched and stained beer glass that Charlie spits into before he polishes it with his dirty shirt. He then pours the juice carefully into the glass and sits there sipping away at it.

Harry laughs. "You gotta laugh," he says to Charlie. Charlie smiles at him. He doesn't really understand what Harry's talking about but it feels good sitting there with Harry laughing and him sipping on his big glass of tuna juice.

It is time now for the serious work to begin. She sees that what she needs is more knowledge, more understanding of the task ahead and that's how she ends up at the library on a Saturday. That's how she sees her homeless man. He's sitting, hunched over, clean earphones over his dirty head. He doesn't see her. Doesn't see anything. His eyes are closed.

It's her intention to sit in the library for as long as she can. She types into the computer, "How to write a symphony." What she finds is mostly sites offering to sell music or sites that contain historical notes about composers. She finds very little that is actually about writing music.

Concentration is not easy to come by. It is far more interesting to study her homeless man than to look through the Internet, which she is finding slow and frustrating. She watches the homeless man and she hopes that he is listening to the CD she has given him. She can hear a faint noise coming from the headphones. She can tell by his face that whatever it is, he is enjoying it. He looks at ease and alive at the same time. He looks happy. She does not think at least she has given him this and this is something, she thinks how much happier he will look when he is listening to music written just for him.

She does find one site of use. A site written by high school students provides her with exactly what she's looking for. The pages show the traditional four-part structure of the symphony and then it breaks the whole thing down into components with musical examples she can listen to.

She makes rapid notes absorbed in her task now that she's found something of use. When she stops to check on her homeless man she finds he has gone. There are still a few hours of daylight left when the library closes so she heads for the beach. She doesn't admit to herself that she's looking for him until she's on the beach, her eyes scouring every corner for the sight of his faded grey coat and his bushy beard.

She finds him in one of the picnic shelters. He's sitting with another man who has bulging plastic bags around him. As she gets closer she can see the can of tuna she bought sitting on the table between them. Its top has been crudely removed and the can is empty. In front of the man with the bags is a glass filled with what looks like dirty water and they're both kind of staring at it.

She stands for a while watching them stare at the glass. Now that she's here she doesn't know what to say. She starts with, "Hi." They direct their stares to her. They do not answer her greeting. She focuses her attention on her homeless man. The other, who switches his attention from her to the glass and back again, scares her more than her homeless man does. She says, "I was hoping I could talk to you."

The one with the bags speaks first. He says, "Is this your daughter Harry?" And she thinks, Harry, his name is Harry. Even if she walks away from this conversation with nothing else, at least she now knows, his name is Harry.

Harry says, "I don't know who she is," and they both keep staring at her. She says, "I'm not your daughter," and Harry says, "Didn't think so." She doesn't know where to start, what she can say next. She feels them both staring and staring. She tries to focus on Harry.

Finally she says, "I saw you one day from the bus. I saw you in your bus shelter and I decided I would write a symphony for you. That's why I left that CD for you. That's why ..."

Harry's face registers the information. There's a shift there as the pieces fall in place for him. His hand slips into his pocket where he's feels the security of the CD within his grasp. He says to her, "So you're a musician then?" and she has to admit that no, not really. The one with the bags cuts in. "How're you going to write a symphony if you're not a musician?" She decides to ignore him. This only makes him speak more. He turns to Harry. "You're a muse Harry. A muse. Who would've thought it?"

Harry looks from his mate to her and he says, "Why?" She answers, "Why what?" because she honestly does not understand what he's asking. He speaks slowly. "Why do you want to write a symphony?" and she is forced to say, "To give you something no one else has." Until she said it she didn't know the reason. But now that she speaks, it seems very clear. Harry takes a while to think about this, as his mate takes a sip from the glass of dirty water.

Eventually Harry says, "I like the one you gave me." She answers, "Wouldn't you like another one?" Harry looks at her for a while and then nods. And that's it. For a moment it's just her and Harry on the beach, no one else. They've crossed a great divide where they have come to stand in each other's worlds and they have told each other what they need to know.

It's time for her to go. She doesn't want to leave now that she and Harry have found this place but she can't think of anything else to say. She tells Harry that she has to go. He nods again. As she is leaving she asks him if there's anything he needs, if there's anything she can get for him. His mate with the bags looks carefully from Harry to her and back again, waiting for Harry to ask for the world but Harry just says, "Next time you buy me a can of food, make it one of them ring pull ones." She feels embarrassed that she didn't think of this before but instead of apologising she nods like Harry. She says, "Sure," and then she leaves.

She feels almost high as she walks back to her apartment. She decides she will call Denis. Perhaps she'll suggest they meet tonight or tomorrow. She'd be able to tell him about her conversation with Harry.

But when she gets home she can't find his phone number. She looks everywhere. Everywhere. She turns her tiny flat upside down and then upside down again. She tries to think. She remembers him handing it to her. She cannot remember what she did with it after that. She remembers smiling. She remembers his eyes. Her pounding heart. But not what she did with his number. She sits down to stare at the mess and think, slowly, carefully. She breathes. Slowly, carefully. That's when she remembers his number was in the pocket of her jeans and her jeans went through the washing machine.

She runs to the pile of clean washing on her bed but it is all too late. There is nothing in her jeans pocket now except a few crumbling pieces of well-washed paper.

She plays the scene again in her head. She sees him hand her his phone number. She tries to watch him write the numbers. Tries to see that slip of paper as it passes from his hand to hers. She tries to visualise the numbers. She remembers a 5 and a 2. Perhaps a couple of 8s. She rubs at her face and hair in frustration. She thought she was being smart to take his number. She was the one taking control and maintaining her personal safety in case he turned out to be some kind of weirdo. But now she has lost him. He has been washed away with the sweat and grime of her clothes.

One day, after clock watching and the library, Harry decides to walk through the university. It was something he used to do a lot because students throw out a lot of good stuff. But it has been a while, he's been distracted with other things so it feels like a whole new adventure when he decides it's time to go back. He takes a new path this day. Harry used to always follow the same path, see the same things. But this day, Harry takes a new path.

Harry, as a young man, had a bit of adventure in him. Just living is usually enough of adventure for him now. But every now and then he wants a little more. So this day he takes a new path through the university to search for the good stuff the students throw away.

He doesn't find anything. Instead he finds a small building. To Harry, it looks like an overgrown hut. It has a glassed-in entrance way with cushioned benches lining the walls. The door is open, inviting Harry in. Inside he sees a plaque. The plaque is cemented into the floor and says 'This foyer was donated by …' Harry spends a long time wondering who would donate a foyer and why.

The foyer is warm, too warm, and the benches look soft and welcoming. It isn't long before Harry is lying down looking at the ceiling of the donated foyer and wondering how many other donated foyers there are around. Whether they are all this warm and comfortable.

Harry is woken by a group of students standing in a semi-circle around his stretched-out body. They scare the shit out of him as they stare and whisper to each other. Some smile a nervous smile, others simply stare. Harry tries to get up, tries to get out of there but there's isn't room. The students are too close, standing too close, watching too close. Harry has to push past, trip over a few feet before he can make his way out of the foyer donated by …

Once outside he turns back to look at them. They are all still standing there, still staring. There are ten, maybe fifteen of them and to Harry they look too young to be away from their mothers' sides. Harry stares back at them, feeling a little safer now there is glass between them. Then he sees that one of them holds a cup. A steaming cup of something. Harry guesses that cup was for him.

But he has gone. Turned away from the university to spend the rest of the day, and some of the night, walking in circles until all becomes a blur of cold and hunger and exhaustion.

Work that week is miserable. She hates it. Hates being there. Hates the students who walk past because they aren't him. She even hates Deanne a bit. Not too much, it's hard to hate Deanne too much. And even though she hates everything, she doesn't want to lose the job.

She finds a moment to sit at one of the pianos but finds it hard to play. The ghosts stand with her, smile encouragingly and wait to hear the scales. But they do not come. She knows this feeling will pass. She knows there will be another day when she will find a room free and she will play. But not this week. This week there is too much to feel bad about. She tries to concentrate on the scale in front of her. It turns out that scales are a lot more complex than she had thought. And impossible to play when you are hating.

So she does as little as she needs to. Enough for Deanne to see progress but not nearly as much as she could do. The rest of the time she sits facing the door and watches the day drag on. The students wander past. She watches those students she has decided to hate as they laugh and sing while walking past and she hates them even more.

The week has nearly ended and she finds herself at home with no desire to sleep. She takes out the notes she made at the library and studies the four parts of a classical symphony. She likes the idea of the four parts. It gives her unwritten symphony a shape. She starts to see it in her mind, this vague swirling shape of music. She concentrates hard remembering that first night with the ghosts where she thought if she really listened closely she'd be able to hear them. But she cannot hear her music, just as she could not hear her ghosts. The swirling shape in her mind remains strong but silent. She gives up trying to hear and lies on the floor, allowing the silent shape of her unwritten symphony to swirl around her.

She wakes some time in the early hours of the morning to find herself still on the floor and crawls to her bed. As she lays her head down on her pillow she hears something that makes her sit up. She hears music. Her music. At first it is a little clumsy and vague but she repeats the sound over and over in her head and it starts to become more defined. She tries to hum the tune but it sounds so terrible out loud that she prefers to leave it in her head. She lies back down because she is very tired and hopes that when she wakes up the music will still be there.

She wakes with an hour before she needs to leave for work no longer hating everything. The music is still there. She tries not to force it, tries to just let it play, but at the same time she feels anxious. She doesn't want to start thinking about something else and find she's lost it. She dresses quickly and heads for the newsagency. She needs a piano in her apartment. She needs to try and find the notes that fit the music in her head.

At the newsagency she pays to use one of the computers installed in the back corner of the shop. She searches the Internet. At first she tries a musicians' page which makes her feel like a fake. She worries someone will come up behind her and shout, "You can't look there, you're not a musician." There is nothing of use in the musicians' section. She turns to general classifieds and finds what she is looking for.

There's a piano for sale for $100. It's a brand she's never heard of in a place she doesn't know but it's a piano for $100. She writes down the phone number. There are baby grands, whites, blacks and walnuts for thousands of dollars. There are ads for stores that are having sales and there's a piano for sale in Marrickville for $250. At least she knows where Marrickville is.

The extras fund is looking pretty good these days. She thinks she could afford a $250 piano. She sees herself catching the train to Marrickville. Then she sees herself on the return journey, the piano on the train next to her. She'd buy it a ticket and drag it home like a pet on a leash.

But then she sees another ad. Free. Piano. Bondi Junction. She writes down the number and the numbers of a few other free pianos listed and then she rushes out the door, late for work.

As she sits on the bus she listens to the music in her head. It's starting to get clearer. She can see herself in her apartment, at her piano, picking out the notes. She sees herself expanding on what's there, playing around with it a little. Beethoven will stand behind her and nod encouragingly. Perhaps he will point her to a note or two. She can see how the little tune in her head will begin to expand into a symphony. She just needs that piano.

She looks out of the bus window and sees that Harry's shelter is empty. Before she completely understands what she is doing she's rung the bell and is waiting impatiently for the bus to stop, for the doors to open. She's going to be late for work. Really late for work. The doors open with a groan and she steps out into the cold and rain all the time thinking she needs to get back on the bus or she'll be late for work.

She runs to the closest supermarket. There she scours the shelves of the canned section trying to think of something Harry would like to eat. It takes more time than she expects. She thought she would come in and grab something and run out again but now she finds she is faced with a number of choices. She ends up reading labels and looking at nutritional values, levels of sodium and fat. She settles on some kind of stew mainly because it has a ring pull. She gets one for herself too because she realises she's forgotten to eat. As she's heading to the checkout she thinks about how the food is going to be eaten and has to run back to the picnic section to buy a packet of plastic forks.

The checkout line is slow and she stands, juggling the two cans and plastic forks in her hands, trying to see what the time is on the watch of the person in front of her. She's late of course, she knows she is but there's nothing she can do about it now. She runs anyway. All the way back to Harry's bus shelter. She's not used to running. By the end she has slowed to a fast walk. At the bus stop she leaves one of the cans and a fork and jumps onto the next bus.

Harry walks, walks until he can't feel his feet any more, but always the same streets, the streets he knows. Harry's shoes are little more than show. The soles are so worn he can feel every sharp stone on the earth beneath him. Still, they stay on his feet, offer some protection against the cold and broken glass.

Sometimes he sits for a bit. Rests his head on his knees. But the cold seeps through and before long Harry is back on his feet, walking those same streets again. Walking, for Harry, has always been a good cure for thinking.

The sun comes up over rooftops and trees and Harry finds he is no longer walking. Instead he kind of leans to the side, towards anything that can support him, a streetlight, a building, a parked car, and then he leans forward and finds that one foot moves to the front to stop him falling. It's slow, but Harry is not in a hurry.

When the sun is well up, Harry rests on a bench in the Junction. He watches people pass, people who have just emerged from their homes, fed and rested, ready for the day ahead. Harry calls to those people as they pass. "What's the time exactly?" Some stop, check their watch or mobile phone and tell him it's 10.05, 10.26, 10.47. But most just keep walking by and Harry doesn't care. Doesn't care at all.

Because by now Harry is asleep on the bench. Dozing in the winter sun. Oblivious to the passing of people and time.

When Harry wakes up and finally makes it back to his bus stop to see the can of food, he's glad it's there because he's hungry and still tired and there's a fork so he doesn't need to think which pocket he put his own in. He just needs to eat. The food in the can doesn't taste that great but Harry keeps eating because he has it in his mind that he just has to get to the bottom of that can and then he will sleep the most beautiful sleep. Before he even gets to see the metal at the bottom he can feel it start to come back up and Harry has to stagger around to the back of the shelter to vomit in the grass.

Only Harry doesn't make it to the grass. He only makes it to the side of his shelter and then everything comes up and onto the footpath looking just like it did in the can only smelling worse. Harry wipes his mouth on his sleeve and chucks the rest of the can in the bushes near the grass. Then he crawls onto the bench in his shelter and tries to get some sleep.

It's unusual for Harry to be in his shelter at this time of day. There is no woman pushing a pram to look forward to. She has long since passed into her day. The morning traffic has passed too. Harry finds the morning traffic soothing. It provides a constant hum. Day traffic stops and starts, stops and starts. Harry tries to sleep but the traffic is not soothing and besides, his guts keep twisting and his head is spinning.

Harry stays lying down but gives up on sleep and watches the traffic instead. A young man pulls his car to a stop in front of the shelter. The car is rough but the stereo is first class and it blares from the windows, not music but talk. The young man in the car taps his fingers in time to the talking and Harry finds that hard to understand. He finds the whole scene hard to understand. To Harry the driver looks 14.

The driver of the car is not 14. He's 22. This is his second car and he is holding down his third job. He feels mature, like a man, and free, like a king, when he drives his car. He does not notice the homeless man sitting at the bus stop squinting at him.

Harry bought his first car when he was 17. He saved the money himself because by then he was working. It was a warehouse job and Harry didn't really understand what they wanted him to do.

A lot of the time he would just sit around. Stare at the floor or the ceiling. Go to the toilet when he wasn't sure what else to do. Then they would call to him, "Move this box, take this to the office." And Harry would do as they said, hating them for the way they spoke to him and the way they didn't. But they would pay him. Not a lot, but something, enough to buy the cheapest car he could find. Harry had always wanted a car.

Deanne is waiting for her when she arrives. She lies. She can't think of anything else to do. She tells Deanne that the bus broke down. That they were told another was on the way but it took half an hour to get to them. Deanne is sympathetic. She catches a bus and a train to get to work every day and home every night so she understands about problems and delays. But she feels bad for lying. Deanne is nothing but nice to her.

She puts the can of stew away to have for lunch and gets on with her day. The work itself is not interesting but she loves to touch all the different sheets of music. She loves to read the names of the composers. The titles of the work. She loves the intricacies of the notes laid out in their bars. She tries to work quickly to make up for her late arrival. Tries not to examine each piece but as the day moves on she finds she works slower and slower. That she examines each piece for longer and longer.

At lunch the stew looks even less appetising than it did in the supermarket. She takes it to the park and finds a dry spot on the grass. She is too embarrassed to eat the can of food in the staff room. She rips off the lid of the can and sticks her plastic fork in. The smell is quite strong so she eats quickly and tries not to think too much about what she is eating.

About half way through the can she notices feet standing near her. She looks up to see Mark standing watching her. She is surprised, embarrassed to be caught with the can of stewed meat in her hand. She asks him, "How long have you been standing there?" and he says, "A while," and asks if the food is any good. She puts the can to the side, as far away as she can and wishes it didn't smell so bad. She asks him what he's doing there. She knows he doesn't work in the area. He says, "I had a meeting nearby. I'm heading back into the office now." He asks how her job is going. How she is.

It's kind of nice to have Mark curious about her life. She should do more to stay in touch. Maybe if they had been closer as children. But they never were. She was the shy older sister. Never sure of herself, never knowing what to do with herself. He was the younger brother. Born with a beauty and a will just to be. She remembers watching him with awe as he grew. As he charged forward into his life. He was the first one to move to Sydney. She followed. Not to be with him. Just because she didn't know what else to do.

She wants to bridge the gap somehow. Let him know she appreciates his interest in her but her eyes are caught by the sight of her student musician.

Denis looks tall and elegant as he strolls through the park. She thinks he moves with a musician's grace although in reality it is probably just the slow stroll of the relaxed 20-something trying not to look too keen. His eyes settle on her and they exchange a smile. She becomes distracted in her conversation with Mark who is trying to arrange to meet her after work.

She tells Mark she'll finish work at six tonight because she was late getting in. He nods like that's a good time for him and suggests a bar they can meet at. She agrees because he is her brother and maybe this will bridge the gap. She also wants him to leave and thinks agreeing will get him to leave sooner. However, agreeing with Mark only makes him feel chattier. He asks her more questions about her job. How long does she think it will last? Will there be more work for her when she's finished the stocktake? She says, "Let's talk about it tonight." She's watching Denis who is now starting to look a little unsure of himself. She can see he doesn't know whether to approach or keep walking.

Mark agrees and heads out of the park, towards the rest of his work day, calling to her that he will see her later and she'd better turn up. She is now free to focus her attention on Denis. Denis watches Mark walk away and then starts to make his way towards her. She feels a sense of excitement and quickly tries to think of something to say. How she will explain the washed out phone number. A voice interrupts her thoughts.

"I like to listen to Puccini on Thursdays." She diverts her attention from Denis to the source of the voice. A short man with a round belly is walking through the park. He says, "Puccini has always sounded like a Thursday to me." He is looking at her as he walks. Looking for a response. She smiles, worried the smile might be an invitation for more conversation on Puccini and Thursdays but unable to think of any other response. And too nervous to ignore him now that they have made eye contact. When she looks back towards where Denis last stood she finds he is no longer there.

A number of thoughts run through her head at this point. She could run after him. He's probably gone back to the school. She could yell at this person who has distracted her and tell him he is a foolish man. Music does not sound like days of the week. She could sit down and cry or eat the remainder of the food not because she is hungry but because then she would not have to smell it any more. She decides on the last option. Eats until she has to scrape the sides of the can, then throws the can and the fork in a bin as she walks back to work.

At work she tries to bring back the music that was in her head when she woke. She looks for Beethoven, thinking he will help her but today she is on her own. The ghosts have stayed home. They are starting to lose interest in her. She is frightened of course. Frightened that the music she heard in her head will never make it to her fingers. That the ghosts have seen this too.

That she will never find the notes and in her failure will realise she can never write a symphony.

She tries to focus on work. Tries to work quickly. Work well. Not think of her missed opportunity to talk to Denis or her symphony. She thinks Deanne will be impressed with how much she has got through today.

Mark is waiting for her at the bar. She's a little surprised. She had half thought he would forget their arrangement and is a bit disappointed because seeing him reminds her of the moment in the park with Denis.

After they get their drinks she tries to tell amusing stories about her new job. She tells him about Deanne and the other staff that she has little to do with. She tells him about the students who sing as they walk the hallways. She tells him about the man in the park after he left her today. About Puccini on a Thursday. Mark shakes his head like he never imagined such people existed. She is pleased with the success of her stories and searches through her memory for more.

At the bar the music is loud and sounds coarse to her ears. She can hear mainly the beat of the drum but little melody. She worries it will drive her own music from her head. Mark picks up the coasters on the table and beats them in a rhythm to the music. She tries to hear when one song ends and another begins but she finds it difficult. It is easier for her to tell when one movement ends and another begins.

Mark leans across the table towards her. His voice is almost a shout so that she can hear. He says, "You know, I've always wondered what the first music was. Where did it come from?" She is impressed by the thought. It's not a question that has ever occurred to her. "Birds?" It's the first thing she thinks of but it seems right to her. Mark leans back in his seat and nods like it's a plausible idea but doesn't really answer his own question.

He goes to buy their second drinks. She wonders how many she is expected to have before she can go home. He brings back the drinks, beer for both of them. She tries not to drink too quickly. Tries to appear relaxed. He leans towards her again. "Is everything all right?" he asks as if he really cares. She understands that this is the point of the evening. To see if she's all right. It begins to dawn on her that their mother has sent him. That he might not even want to be there. Asking this question.

She remembers a few phone calls lately that she has not bothered to answer. A couple of messages on her machine from her mother that she has forgotten to return.

And then there is the question itself. Even if he has been requested to ask it. It makes her want to cry. Of course she's not all right. She's lonely. Lost. Desperate to find a place where she belongs, where she feels useful. She doesn't want to cry. Not here, not now, not in front of Mark. And she doesn't. But he can see she's upset. She can't speak. So he speaks for her.

"I can see you're upset. I can see you're lonely. I'm worried about you."

She thinks if he hadn't come to find her today perhaps she would be sitting here with Denis. Perhaps then she wouldn't be feeling so lonely.

She finds herself getting a little angry. Mark has no right to intrude in her life like this. To make judgements, compare his life to hers. Her mother, she's sure now it's her mother that's sent him, has no right to be doing this either. She finishes her drink, gathers her things.

"I'm fine. Tired from work, but I'm fine. Thanks for the drinks. Sorry I can't stay for another. I really have to go."

She kisses him on the cheek to show him how fine she is and then she walks out of the bar towards the nearby bus stop. She is fine she tells herself. Or she will be. All she can do is keep going. If she keeps going she'll be fine.

Mark yelled, "Call me," as she walked away from the bar but she thinks, "No, no I won't." She cannot pollute her mind with beer and dance music. She cannot have someone who reminds her how lonely and miserable she really is. She can only keep going. Get a piano. Maybe when she has that piano, when the music in her head has been turned into notes, maybe then she'll call him.

FOURTH

That car. Harry loved it. It wasn't much to look at of course but Harry found it comfortable inside. So comfortable he almost lived it in. The back seat was full of clothes and magazines, the front full of drink bottles and cassettes to listen to.

Every Saturday Harry would be off. Mostly with no idea about where he was going. He'd drive so far he'd have to sleep in the back seat, covered by the extra clothes if it was a cold night and with the windows open and his feet sticking out if it was hot. At first his mother was mad, she didn't like him disappearing like he did. She'd stay up all night waiting for the police to knock on the door and say there'd been an accident. Stay up until sometime after lunch when Harry would appear, then she would yell, then sleep. The next weekend they would do it all over again.

Harry drove that car everywhere. He covered the state looking for places he'd never been, hoping he would find somewhere no one else had found. Sometimes hoping he would find people, people just like him who he could talk to and laugh with. Perhaps live with. And sometimes he did. Sometimes he found people right when he needed to. They would spend the night drinking and laughing, telling stories that were only half true. But in the morning they would all go their own way. And Harry would be left to start again. To find a new road. He drove that car everywhere he could, anywhere there was a road, and once, on that last Saturday, where there wasn't.

It's time to give up on the bus shelter. Sleep refuses to come to Harry and reminiscing is a dangerous sport for him. So Harry swings his legs down towards the ground and pulls himself upright. He closes his eyes, sits still for a moment but his head spins. He considers vomiting again and his body aches with tiredness. Harry ignores his body and stands.

He heads off down the street, hands in his pockets, eyes on the ground. He tries not to think. Tries not to feel. It's no use of course. His body screams at him with aches and pains and discomfort. His mind reels from his body to his memories to the girl. The symphony girl.

The library stands opposite Harry. Just across the road that is swaying in front of Harry's eyes. Harry stares at the library. He tries to still the road. If the road were to stay still then perhaps he could cross it but the road will not stay still. The cars will not stop coming and Harry decides it would be easier to just keep walking. Perhaps the sight and smell of the ocean will make him feel better.

The road to the beach is quite long but pretty much all downhill. Harry feels he is not so much walking as falling towards the beach. He leans his body forward and then his feet stumble out in front to stop him hitting the ground. This is the method he employs and he stops for no one. Cars, people, they are all required to get out of his way today. Fortunately they do because Harry cannot stop now that he has started, not until he has the water in his sights.

And when he does see that tremendous stretch of blue and grey he begins to feel better. He starts to walk properly, with his head held high, he starts to watch for traffic and avoid other pedestrians. The ground becomes more solid under his feet and he begins to feel like company.

The first person Harry sees is Charlie because Charlie is easy to see from a distance. Then, as Harry gets closer, he sees others. Others whose names are not familiar to him but who he feels he knows somehow. One of the others holds a brown paper bag.

A younger man than Harry. He calls a greeting and invites Harry to share in that brown paper bag.

Normally Harry would not touch the stuff. It's the death of you on the street. That's what Harry was told. That's what Harry says. That's what Harry believes. But today. Well, today is a little different. And maybe it will help Harry to sleep.

So Harry takes the brown paper bag the young man offers and he feels the bottle beneath the paper. He sits with the men and he touches the bottle to his lips. Before he drinks he feels it important to make things clear. So he says, "Normally I don't touch this stuff." And the men nod like they already knew this to be the case. Like they understand that today is different. Then Harry feels it's all right to take a swig so he takes a big one. It tastes lousy and burns all the way down, which somehow makes Harry feel pretty good. So he takes another swig before he hands it back around.

Soon Harry is no longer thinking. He is close to not feeling. He can enjoy the wind and the salt in the air. He can enjoy the company of the men he is with. He thinks soon he will feel so good he will be able to walk back to his shelter and get some sleep. Then he will wake up in the morning and everything will be fine again.

But this is not what happens. The day ends quickly and Harry finds he is too tired to walk up the hill to his shelter. Harry finds that where he is right now is just fine for sleeping and that being in the company of these men is a comfort. So Harry settles down with the others. Sure they swear a little at each other but they all sleep there and in the morning they sit again and continue their talking.

It turns out that the free piano in Bondi Junction is still in Bondi Junction and is still free. They say it works fine, just takes up too much space, gathers dust. She takes their address, asks them to hold it for her. Tells them she'll pick it up, as soon as she can arrange it. However getting a free piano delivered is expensive. Far more expensive than she was anticipating. She tries to think of another way and the removalists tell her she can push it, put it on a little trolley and push it down the street, carry it up the stairs, play it out of tune. They think they're being funny but she starts to think it's a good idea.

She heads first to the hardware store to get a trolley. It's not cheap but cheaper than the delivery truck and they offer to loan it to her for a fee rather than making her buy it. Then she heads for the beach because she thinks that's where he'll be. The sky is grey but the clouds look light and she doesn't believe they hold the promise of rain. She continues to glance up at them as she searches for Harry. Rain would ruin her plan.

Then the symphony girl appears and she starts to talk about pushing a piano from the Junction back to the beach and the men sitting with Harry are nodding their heads like they think it's a great idea. Harry is left with a great fog in his brain trying to work out how to slip quietly away. The men gather around Harry and start shuffling forward. Harry has no choice but to shuffle along with them. Soon he is walking back up that hill but not to his shelter.

She is pleased that the men are following her. Harry doesn't look pleased but she ignores it and tells him, "Thank you for helping, Harry." He looks even more unhappy to hear that he is going to be helping. She tells him about the piano and how she needs it to write his symphony but it's in the Junction and too expensive to have delivered. The men around Harry are nodding like they know how expensive it is to get pianos delivered and they all give Harry a bit of a nudge until he agrees that helping is the right thing to do. The men agree to help too. All but the one with the bags. He moves away from the group when there is talk of helping. A few more drop off as they walk up the hill.

In total there are four of them, including her, now heading towards the Junction. Harry walks closest to her because the others seem to make him. He hasn't spoken yet and she wonders what he is thinking. He stares at his feet as he walks and keeps pace with her. There is no invitation from him to talk so she stays silent until they get to the main road.

At the main road she announces that they should take the bus and that she will pay. The other two loudly agree it's a good idea. Harry continues to stare at his feet. A bus arrives quickly and she ignores the look of the driver and other passengers as she pays for the four of them. There is some question of sitting or standing between them and in the end they all stand and dot themselves out along the aisle of the bus. This removes the need to talk and disperses their smell throughout the entire bus.

It's not a terrible gagging kind of smell but it is an ever-present odour. A smell of nights slept outside, of clothing and bodies unwashed. It's the kind of smell that would make you feel claustrophobic if you were in a confined, still space. With the bus moving the smell is bearable. A reminder that these men standing on the bus lead very different lives to those sitting. But a smell not strong enough to make those sitting feel they need to do anything about it.

The ghosts have joined them on the bus. They position themselves among the other passengers. Some standing, others sitting where there are seats to spare or laps available. She can feel their excitement, their pleasure in seeing her take such a decisive step towards writing her symphony.

She uses the time on the bus to examine the men she has brought with her. One of them looks young, maybe even her age or younger. He wears a suit, brown with a pinstripe. The cuffs of the jacket are fraying a little and there are a few stains around the place but all in all it looks to be in quite good condition. She thinks that if she does need to take one of them into the house with her then he would be the one. Under the suit he has a bulky blue jumper and when she looks down to his feet she sees that they are bare. The skin on the top of his feet is red, the feet look raw and sore. He has thin bits of facial hair on his chin and lips and around his jaw. When he catches her looking at him he smiles which allows her to see how bad his teeth are. She returns the smile and turns to look out the window.

The other man is shorter and a little round. He looks Italian and she finds it hard to guess his age. Maybe forty but he could be ten years either side of it. If he was asked the question he would not tell. Not because he can't remember – he remembers his birth date well – but because he would view anyone wanting to know with great suspicion.

He is dressed much like Harry, a mismatch of pants and shirts with a large overcoat. The clothing is well worn like Harry's but unlike Harry, this man is clean shaven. This is because he shaves every day, it's important to him. He may sometimes feed himself from the inside of a garbage bin and sleep wherever he can find shelter but his face will always be clean shaven.

At the Junction she directs them all from the bus and through the streets to the address she was given. Every now and then she turns to make sure they are still following. The ghosts skip and dance alongside the homeless men. The young man gives her an encouraging smile every time she turns and it helps her to keep moving forward.

The people giving away the piano find it a little hard to believe she is really going to push it home. She shows them the trolley and the men standing at the gate, ready to help and so they shrug and help her manoeuvre the piano onto the trolley and out of their house, grateful to see it leaving through their door.

It was bound to happen of course. No one gives and gives and asks nothing in return. Even Bloody Brian wants something from Harry. And the girl … Harry doesn't know exactly what the girl wants from him but he can start to see a long line of chores ahead. Expected from him because he took the music, took the food. Harry should have seen this coming. Should have refused all she offered. Harry is not in the habit of helping other people.

Compared to the pianos at the school, this piano is not much to look at. The wood is worn and scratched. A piece of the ivory, or plastic more likely, is missing from one of the top D keys. Others are chipped or cracked. It is, however, a piano and she is keen to have it in her apartment.

The young homeless man claps as she appears on the footpath with the piano. He suggests she plays a tune. She shakes her head, pretends he's joking. They take their positions around the piano and begin to push.

People stare of course. They stand to one side to make way and then they stay there and watch as they continue on. Only a few hurry around them like the sight of three homeless men and one woman pushing a piano is something they see every day. She wonders how much more they would stare if they, like her, could see the small army of ghosts, pushing with them.

They push the piano out of the Junction and up the hill. They push it past Harry's bus stop and over streets. At the Council chambers they stop to catch their breath. They stare down the sloping road ahead of them. At the end they can see the water of the ocean. It's grey today, reflecting the clouds in the sky. She looks up and wills the rain to stay away.

It's hard work. There are times she wants to give up. Times when she would be happy to leave the piano by the side of the road, go home and forget all about it. She looks at the three men positioned around the piano and wonders why they continue to help and what she'll do when they give up.

She thought pushing the piano downhill would be easier than

pushing it up but actually it isn't. She and Harry have to anchor it from behind while the other two try to control it from the front and in this way they struggle down the hill. Cars slow down to watch, some pedestrians clap, others help for short distances. She thinks it could possibly be fun if it wasn't such hard work and she wasn't so terrified of being left alone on the street with a piano.

Once they are off the main road they decide to push it on the road rather than the footpath which is uneven and difficult. Now instead of pedestrians stopping to stare they have cars swerving and tooting. It's not easy keeping the piano in a straight line and they are all so tired that they are not trying any more. She still thinks of giving up. And is more and more grateful that the three men do not.

They make it to the base of her apartment and it's there she realises she hasn't really thought this through. Her block has a lift. A small, slow, tired lift but a lift so at least there are no stairs. They shove the piano into the lift and then try to position themselves around it. No one wants to take the stairs. And it is there, crammed into the lift with the piano and three homeless men that she starts to question the wisdom of bringing these men into her home.

In the lift the odour of the four sweating bodies becomes unbearable. When the doors open onto her floor they spill from the lift in relief and shove the piano out into the hall. Out of the lift Harry stands, half resting on the piano. The younger man slumps against the nearest wall and the third falls to the floor, lying on his back. The ghosts pace impatiently. They want the piano in the apartment, safe behind her closed door.

She opens her apartment door and returns with water. She promises them food as soon as the piano is safely in her apartment as a way to get them moving. The men return to their feet. They lean against the piano and it moves slowly into her apartment. She is happy to have it in the middle of the room but getting the trolley out from under it takes some time.

She would like to stay now that she has the piano. Would like to sit down and try it straight away. But it's a little too strange, a little too scary to be standing there with three homeless men so she heads for the door and invites them out for food. They all stand silently in the lift, each one trying not to inhale until they get out into the open air.

Once outside, the men head straight for the beach where they can lie on the grass. She walks to the nearest fish and chip shop and orders four. She thinks it would look rude if she gave them the food and her thanks and then walked off back to her warmer apartment for a shower and some fresh clothes.

She sits awkwardly with the men as they eat their food. She eats as fast as she can, desperate to get to her piano. The men eat quickly too. She doesn't know whether they are just hungry or if they too are desperate to get away from her. The conversation is stilted despite their efforts to recount their afternoon achievements. She tries to thank them. Tries to say how much she appreciates their help. When she feels she can, she stands and says another clumsy thankyou and goodbye. It's not enough, she knows it's not enough, but she doesn't know what else she can do. The men barely look up as she leaves.

It is almost a relief when the younger one chases her to ask for money. She gives him what she has in her pocket and he seems happy enough with it. She does not have time to wonder if she has now set herself up as the money-giving woman but even if she has, this is a small price to pay for having that piano, all hers and sitting, waiting for her, in the middle of her apartment. Besides, they have seen her apartment now and know she doesn't have much. Still more than them, but not that much.

At home she rushes through the shower and into fresh clothes. Her body aches as she moves but she understands it's important that she keep going. As she is walking to the piano the phone rings. She considers not answering it but remembers the evening with Mark. She remembers the messages from her mother that she has forgotten to respond to. For a brief moment she thinks it could be Denis. That somehow he's found her number and is calling because he hasn't heard from her. Because he saw her in the park that day but wasn't sure whether to talk to her. Because he can't stop thinking about her.

She picks up the phone. It's her mother. She tries to sound calm and patient. She tries not to sound too tired or annoyed. She tells her mother about her job. About Deanne. She asks questions. About her mother. About her father. About the weather. She watches the ghosts at the piano and wishes she could move her hands the way they do. Sit with the poise that they have.

When she feels she can she says that she needs to go. Her mother doesn't mind. She doesn't like long conversations on the phone. She just wants to know her daughter is all right.

Harry watches the young bloke come back from chasing the symphony girl, grinning with a fist full of money. He is jubilant. Excited by their adventure and the cash and food they've gained from it. He talks of setting up a furniture removal business. An environmentally friendly one because all the moving would be done by foot. No one else thinks this is a good idea. He doesn't care. He announces that tonight is a party night.

Harry watches him again as he runs off to the pub and wonders where he gets his energy. He tries to remember if he had that kind of energy at his age and then realises he doesn't care and brings his focus back to the remainder of his food. Tony is beside him, already finished. He looks ready to fall asleep.

The young bloke returns with some of his chips still in hand and a bottle of grog. He starts a furious exercise in alternating between shoving food in and gulping drink down. By now Harry has nothing at all to lose so he takes the bottle when it's offered. Tony does the same and before long all of the food is gone and the bottle is mostly empty.

Harry is kind of floating above the grass. He doesn't feel the cold even though he knows it's there. He lies still and he stares at nothing in particular. He becomes completely unaware of his surroundings. He no longer knows if anyone is with him. He no longer understands if he is asleep or awake. He only knows that he is resting.

The piano is horribly out of tune. She plays it anyway. Not for long on that first night, she is too tired to sit up for long. But the next day she plays. She plays most of the day and even though the lack of tune kind of hurts her ears, she can't help but touch the keys. Some of ghosts are horrified when they hear her play the out of tune piano. They up and leave like this is the final insult in a string of insults they've had to endure.

She ignores their departure. Instead she looks to Beethoven for his encouraging smile. She practises her scales. They have not improved greatly. It disappoints her. She had thought she'd be a natural. Thought that she'd learn quickly, almost instantaneously. Thought she would remember each and every scale. Thought they would become a part of her. But the reality is that she must keep studying the book. The reality is that her fingers do not keep in time with each other and she needs to go over and over the same scale to get one perfect out of tune rendition. She stumbles over the more complex scales and rarely gets them right.

She can still hear the music in her head. The music she believes to be hers. When she gives up on the scales she spends some time listening to the CDs she owns to see if she can find her music within those pieces. But so far the music in her head seems to be really hers. Yet when she sits at the piano to find the notes, they elude her. She returns to scales where the notes are already safely written.

As she plays the scales she thinks about buying paper. She is sure that soon she will find those notes and when she does she wants to write them down. Wants to capture them on paper so they can't escape. She remembers reading that Schubert drew his own lines. She likes this idea. Perhaps she too will draw her lines. Then all she needs is blank paper. She likes the idea of starting with a perfect blank page and gradually filling it with music.

On Monday she returns to work with new energy and still sore legs from moving the piano. She arrives early and sneaks into one of the piano rooms, hoping that an in-tune piano might help her find the notes in her head. She closes her eyes to see if this will help her find those notes. She feels someone sit beside her on the piano stool. She turns to see who it is, hoping, hoping that it is not Deanne. She doesn't know what she would say to Deanne.

It's Denis.

She feels so happy she wants to scream. Instead she giggles a bit. She can't help it. She feels like a fool sitting there smiling and giggling at him. He says, "How's it going?" just as she says, "I washed your phone number with my jeans," and then they both just sit there for a while smiling at each other.

At first their conversation is stilted. They talk over one another or pause for long periods of time but soon enough they find their own rhythm and the conversation starts to flow. It's been a long time since she felt so happy. Denis tells her about his studies and she tells him about the piano now sitting in her apartment, out of tune, but there. Denis nods his head like it's entirely possible for her to write a symphony on her free, homeless men-delivered, out-of-tune piano. Denis has a friend who knows how to tune pianos. He offers to ask him to come and tune hers. He tells her his friend will work for beer and when she asks, "When?" he says, "Any time." She says, "After work?" without properly thinking about whether it's safe to invite this person and his friend into her apartment.

She imagines her mother telling her she is taking too many risks, first the homeless men and now Denis and his friend. Her mother would not believe her unwritten symphony is worth these risks and she starts to feel nervous. It's too late though because Denis is already making plans to contact his friend and meet her at her apartment. She feels she has no choice but to write down her address and when he says "Goodbye," and "See you later," she feels both excitement and dread.

On her way home she shops for food and beer. She has not been home long before there is a knock at her door and Denis is in her apartment introducing her to his friend. He has also brought beer. His friend carries a small case with the tools he needs to tune the piano. He chats briefly, eats some of the food she offers and takes a beer to the piano. When he plays a scale he whistles like he hasn't heard anything so bad in a long time. She worries he won't be able to tune the piano but he seems to take it as a challenge and settles down to work.

Denis keeps looking at her, smiling at her. She can't help smiling back even though her heart is pounding and she's starting to feel a little sick. He doesn't seem to think her apartment is strange with the bareness of it and the piano sitting awkwardly in the middle of the tiny room. With the photocopied images of the composers staring from the walls.

The piano tuner becomes completely focused on the task and she begins to feel like he's unaware that she and Denis are there too. She would like to get in close to see what he's doing. But his concentration is so intense she feels she can not disturb him. So she sits on the couch with Denis and sips her beer, watching as he works. Occasionally they bring him food, or give him a new beer, and he takes it, looks their way briefly and smiles like he's surprised to see them there. Denis assures her that this is fun for his friend. That it is fun for him also to be there watching, with her, but she finds herself apologising for how badly out of tune the piano is, for the cracked keys and the scratched woodwork, for how late it is getting.

And then it is dark. Really dark. And cold. Really cold. It's time to get up and get moving but Harry finds he can't. All he can do is lie there, staring at the sky. Harry can make out clouds above him in the night sky. There is an occasional star that blinks at him between the clouds. This convinces him he is not dead.

Harry thinks perhaps trying to get up was starting too big so he starts small. He tries moving his toes. They move. Slowly, painfully but they move. He tries his fingers. There is a burning pain that radiates up his arms as he slowly bends and straightens his digits. Harry starts to feel encouraged. He is warmed by the burning feeling and embraces the pain because at least he is now feeling something.

He moves his head from side to side. This brings on a fresh bout of pain, worse this time. Not warming at all. Harry lies still. He feels his breath enter and leave his body. He looks for stars in the sky. He listens for gulls on the beach. There is the gentle lap of the ocean. There is the sound of cars. The stars disappear behind clouds. The gulls are quiet.

Harry thinks if he cannot move he will die and decides to get up. It surprises him a little that he has decided not to die. That he doesn't think "Enough is enough," and to let the cold take him. He rolls awkwardly onto his front and bends his knees under him. His chest and head is hardest to get off the ground but when he does he finds he can sit upright and catch his breath before learning forward again to use his hands. Suddenly the ground is once again beneath Harry's feet and Harry, staggering and stumbling, is moving.

He doesn't make it far, but he makes it to a shelter. The relative warmth of a wooden bench and the limited protection of a thin roof overhead. Harry lies down and waits for morning.

She wakes to a gentle shaking from Denis. She sits quickly, startled, embarrassed. Denis apologises, he thinks he's scared her. He apologises for how long the tuning has taken and she apologises for falling asleep and for keeping him up so late. Denis laughs and suggests they stop apologising. She agrees but still feels the need to apologise a little more. Denis tells her the piano is tuned to the best of his friend's ability and that they are going to go now so she can get some more sleep. She nods obediently, relieved that they are going, that Denis expects nothing more from her. Disappointed that he is going, that he expects nothing more from her.

At the door he asks her if she'd like to go out with him some time and she says that she would. He says, "Good," and then he is gone and it's only when she's climbing into her bed that she realises they didn't swap phone numbers or make any real plans to see each other again.

Morning comes slowly, like it would prefer not to come at all. It brings no warmth. Harry dozes on and off as he waits for the full light of day. Then he starts again. Toes, fingers, head, rolling into a sitting position. This time Harry waits a while. He lets the spinning in his head subside before he even thinks of standing. And then he is up and moving. He walks quickly. If he stops he may fall.

On his way he calls to people, "What's the time exactly?" Nobody answers. All the way to the main road, nobody answers. Harry sits at the edge of the road, his feet in the gutter. He leans into a nearby post. There is a little sun now, a little warming sun. A man crossing the road tells Harry it's 8.15 am. Early.

Harry walks some more. The street becomes busy with pedestrian traffic and Harry finds himself rolling into them, pushing away from them to give himself momentum to get up the hill. The people Harry touches feel warm, like there's a heater somewhere in their jackets. Harry is still cold from the ground, cold from the drink.

Harry stands outside the library. It would be warm in the library. There would be a smiling woman, possibly a hot drink. Harry sees himself comfortable, falling asleep with the sound of Beethoven in his ears and a warm drink clasped in his hands. He'd never want to leave and the smiling woman would end up having to kick him out and then he wouldn't be able to come back. Once you get kicked out of a place they don't like you coming back. Isn't that what she said? Don't come back. All those years ago. That's what she said. And Harry listened.

And now, if the smiling woman said that to him that would be the end, there'd be no more Beethoven.

Harry continues up the hill. It's not so far to his bus stop now.

At the bus stop there are people sitting on the bench. Harry sits with them. He tries to stretch out but there isn't the room and the people sitting aren't interested in moving for him. He asks them, "What's the time exactly?" They stand up without answering and get on a bus. They try not to look at him. Not until they are safely on the bus, with the glass between them do they look at Harry and then they stare and stare as Harry stretches out and the bus moves away.

Harry sleeps. He sleeps all day, waking to note the passing of the day, and then falling asleep again. It still hurts to move so he stays still. He listens to the traffic and then he sleeps again. The street is quiet. He has missed clock watching. Not once, but twice. It's been a long time since Harry missed clock watching. The night is long and Harry is wide awake. He has a lot of time to think about what bad thing is about to happen.

When she wakes up she sits at the piano before doing anything else. She starts with the C scale, then G, then D. The tuned piano sounds so much better. It encourages her to play better than she's ever played before. She plays scales until her fingers hurt, her bladder is aching and her stomach is gnawing at her from the inside. She doesn't try to find the notes in her head. She tells herself that she's familiarising herself with the piano. That she's working up to it. She plays the scale of A.

After E she manages to tear herself away to go to the toilet and make some toast. It is there that she sees the time. If she doesn't leave now she'll be late for work again. She gets ready and just as she's about to walk out the door she pauses. She plays another scale standing up. She plays it again. She sits down to have another go. She plays around the scale, trying different notes to see if she can find a tune. Not her tune, just a tune, any tune. Then she runs out the door and to the bus. The few ghosts that have remained with her opt to stay home with the piano rather than join her at work.

She runs as fast as she can but running makes no difference. She's late again.

When she arrives at work she expects the worst. She expects Deanne to be cross. To tell her to leave and not to come back. But Deanne isn't there. And when Deanne does turn up she only looks relieved. Only seems pleased to see her. She tells Deanne, "I was late. I was worried you'd be cross." And Deanne smiles at her. Tells her she knows that she was late. That she's glad she came. That some days she worries that the work is so dull that she will leave and not come back the next day and then Deanne will be stuck having to do the dull work.

Deanne tells her it doesn't matter what time she comes in. As long as she does her hours. Does the job. That's all she cares about. She tries to tell Deanne how much she likes the job but Deanne won't listen. Can't believe anyone would enjoy being stuck in a room meticulously going through music sheet by sheet.

As she works she keeps one ear to the sounds outside the door. One ear listening for Denis. And when she hears steps just before lunch she knows they are his. Her heart beats with anticipation and she looks at the music in her hands so that she doesn't look like she was waiting for him. Denis walks into the room looking lean and lovely and like he got plenty of sleep. She hopes she looks the same. Seeing him all the tiredness she felt when she got out of bed vanishes and she feels excitement. Excitement and joy.

Denis suggests they go to lunch and this seems perfect because she has forgotten to bring any. They walk to a nearby café that sells cheap soups and they sit side by side waiting for their food. Their legs and hips touch as they sit and she is desperate to lean towards him. To feel more of his body against hers.

Their conversation flows easily as they exchange details of their lives. Where they grew up, siblings. Topics that for some reason were not covered last night when they watched the piano getting tuned.

When the food arrives the conversation becomes more awkward and she feels self-conscious eating in front of him. They move slightly apart needing elbow room to spoon the soup into their mouths. She tries hard not to slurp. Denis makes a joke of it. Slurping loudly and scraping his spoon over the bowl. Shaking his head with the wrongness of his idea to go for soup. She laughs. She finds him charming.

As they walk back to the school Denis lets his hand brush

hers and she in turn lets hers brush his. Just before the school they pause, Denis holds her back. She needs to get back to work but she cannot resist staying longer with him. He asks if she would mind if he kissed her and she nods and smiles as her stomach tightens in excitement and his lips move towards hers.

    It is not long enough. Not nearly long enough but all the time she has. She drags herself away from him and goes back to work. The smile is still on her face.

There is no question in Harry's mind that a bad thing is going to happen. You miss clock watching, you pay the price. It is the wonder of which bad thing it will be that keeps Harry wide awake and fretting. There are a lot of possibilities.

Morning comes as reluctantly as it did the day before. It comes without sun and without the passing of the pram. Harry dozes to the sound of morning traffic and then, when it seems to be time, he makes his way to the Junction. He asks every person he sees, "What's the time exactly?" He stands in front of them so they can't leave without telling him so they say, 9.58, 10.03, 10.04, 10.05. He says exactly again when they say quarter past, half past. Then they say 10.17, 10.29.

Harry has never clock watched so well. By 11.00 he is ready to sleep again, exhausted from his work. But Harry's aching body needs a shower so he heads to the beach.

Everything hurts as he walks to the beach. Harry tries to accommodate the pain. He watches it as he walks. The stiffness, the aching, the occasional sharp jabs. He finds his body will move in spite of it all and that walking is easier if he concentrates only on his body and forgets anything that is outside of it.

The day is grey but still and Harry is grateful for the stillness. For that lack of cold wind that does not rip through his bones. He looks to the skies and is hopeful that they will keep him warm today. That they will not rain on him. He thinks he has done a good job clock watching today. Maybe good enough to have a warm day. Maybe even good enough to stop bad things from happening.

Tony is at the showers. He is damp and pink when Harry arrives. The two men acknowledge each other with a nod because they are past the need for words. Harry tries to see if Tony is as stiff as he is without appearing to stare. It would be good to think it was all down to the piano moving. If all this pain was only from physical exertion then Harry would know that in a few days it would be gone, forgotten, remembered only as a passing phase.

Tony is sitting still with his head against the wall behind him. Harry thinks to ask him, does your body hurt like mine? But the idea of warmth from the shower pulls Harry towards it before he can form the words. He strips off his clothes and puts them in a neat pile where he can grab them before anyone else does, because you never know what sort of thieves and idiots are around waiting to leave a man naked in the public showers. Then he turns the hot water on as hard as it can go and stands beneath it trying to imagine the pain draining away.

When Harry can avoid it no longer he gets out of the shower. He uses one of his shirts to dry off quickly and he tries to move like there is no pain because Tony is still sitting there. His clothes, dirty and cold, go on with difficulty and stick to his damp skin, twisting and tightening around his limbs.

Then he starts to cough.

The coughing fills Harry's mouth so he spits onto the floor. The floor between where he is standing and where Tony is sitting. He doesn't think about it. Just spits. And there it is. Blood. A bright mess of blood that has come out of Harry's mouth and landed on the floor. It scares Harry. It scares Tony too. The men stare and stare at that bright blood on the floor. Harry looks at Tony to see if he's noticed and Tony is just staring and staring. Staring at it but not talking about it. Harry is grateful for that.

Tony tries to make conversation about other things. He talks and Harry tries to respond but still they stare at the blood on the floor. It is hard for Harry to understand the words passing between them.

It seems that Tony is going to Perth to escape the coming Olympics. He's saying he's all cleaned up for his big trip. Harry agrees. It's a big trip. Tony smiles. It's not a happy smile. Harry can't work out what kind of smile it is. Tony says he's not hanging around Sydney waiting for the Olympics to ruin everything.

Harry leaves Tony in the showers, still sitting there, still staring at the blood on the floor. Harry can't be near that blood any more. He needs to be at the library. It's a slow walk up the hill. Harry tries to focus on the smiling woman and what she might offer today. It is better than thinking about the blood on the floor. He and Tony staring and not knowing what to say.

At the library there is no smiling woman. Instead there's a man. Not the Saturday man. A different man. A man who doesn't look up from what he's reading when Harry comes in. A man who still doesn't look up even when Harry is standing right in front of him. Waiting for him to notice. Harry has to clear his throat. He does it with as much delicacy as he can. He does not want to spit blood in the library. The man looks up and then, just for a moment, he looks scared.

It is amusing for Harry, still after all these years, to watch the shake in the man's hand as he passes the headphones to him. It makes Harry feel a little taller. A little larger. The man looks as if he wants to go wash his hands. Harry doesn't care. He's starting to feel a little better.

There's no one at the computers. Harry had assumed the symphony girl would be there. He has gotten used to seeing her around. Almost expects her to be behind him when he turns or in front of him when he's walking down the street. But she's not in the library and that's good too.

The chair is the most comfortable thing Harry's sat on for a while. He slides the CD into its slot in the computer and settles back with the headphones on his ears. The music fills him. He closes his eyes and tries to imagine the music washing the pain from his body. For a while it works. For a while there is no pain. In fact for a while there is no Harry. He's not in his body. Not in the library. He is nowhere and there is no pain.

A lull in the music brings him back and he finds his head is spinning and his eyes have trouble focusing. He breaks out in a sweat and a foul taste fills his mouth. Harry takes the CD from the computer as fast as he can. He leaves the headphones where they are and keeps his mouth clamped shut. Once outside the library Harry lies down on the cool footpath and lets his stomach empty itself of nothing but foul tasting bile. Then everything stops for a while.

It is early when she wakes. Or at least early for her and she feels ready. But she delays. Holds herself back. Showers and eats breakfast, slow mouthfuls of toast which she enjoys for as long as she can. She walks to the piano with unhurried confidence and sits down knowing that today the music will come. She pushes the ghosts to the side and she closes her eyes. She listens to the music in her head and imagines it travelling down through her neck, into her shoulders, past her elbows until it arrives at her fingers. She opens her eyes and positions her fingers lightly on the keys.

She had expected it would work. She had expected her symphony would suddenly appear through this short meditation. Like destiny. Like it was meant to be. But it doesn't. Not as she had hoped. Not as the complete form she has expected to appear. There are notes, here and there. She finds notes that fit the notes in her head and she knows that she needs to be happy with this. That this is the start of Harry's symphony.

She stays at the piano for as long as she dares. At work she stops at one of the piano rooms. Plays her notes again. She plays them over and over. Fast then slow. She plays them until she finds a rhythm that works. Then she tries to take the notes further. She tries to take them somewhere other than where they sit in her head. She finds a couple more notes. Then she goes back to work.

She finds it hard to concentrate on the music in her hands, the list on the computer. She is still thinking about her notes, amazed that she is not thinking about Denis. She finds a piece of scrap paper and draws the shape of the full symphony. She tries to see the music with her eyes closed. She draws an arc, a curve of music, building, falling, rising again. She adds a few dips for interest and doesn't think about how she is going to make that arc happen, just sees it as there, as right.

Denis enters the room while she has her eyes closed concentrating on the fuzzy shape before her. She opens her eyes to see him standing quietly, watching her. The music falls out of her head as soon as she sees him. She doesn't care. She smiles at Denis and it is like he has always been there. Always been a part of her life. And then she looks again and he seems brand new.

He wants to kiss her. She can tell that he wants to kiss her. He asks her how the piano is sounding. She thanks him again for arranging the tuning and he brushes her thanks aside as he asks her to have coffee with him after she finishes work. She says yes despite feeling tired, despite the big part of her that wants to go home and play those first found notes of her symphony all over again. She says yes because she finds him very attractive and she thinks he might feel the same about her. She says yes because he knows about music and perhaps he can help her. She says yes because she is lonely and he is there offering her something more.

Denis is waiting outside the school for her when she finishes work for the day. They walk towards Oxford Street, to a place she has never been before, a place that seems more for travellers than locals. A place that is warm and dark, with drip filter coffee and a limited menu. They sit across the table from one another waiting for their coffee to arrive. Denis asks her whether she is enjoying the piano and she has no hesitation in telling him about her symphony. She tells him about Harry and about finding some notes this morning. She describes the process of hearing the music in her head, of encouraging it into her fingers. She tells him about the fuzzy shape of the full symphony that is now floating before her. She talks about the classic four-part structure, how she's going to use it, just like Beethoven did. She ends by thanking him again for helping her get the piano tuned. She can't stop thanking him for this.

As she talks Denis watches. He nods his head. He does not laugh. He just listens and when she's finished he says that it sounds like she's making good progress and suggests she could play it to him one day. She says she's not ready to share it yet and he nods again like he understands.

Denis started playing the piano when he was three. His mother was a music teacher and she taught him until he became too good. Then he went to other music teachers. As he tells her this she thinks about where she would be if she had started playing the piano at three. How many symphonies could she have written? Or would she just have moved away from music, the way she has with everything else?

On her way home she thinks about Harry. She has not invited Denis home despite their long kiss goodbye. Despite her loneliness. She feels confident that she will see him again. Confident that he wants to spend time with her and that he is the right person to be with as she writes her symphony. She feels confident that not inviting him home does not mean that she's turned him away.

So she thinks about Harry. She thinks about what his life could have been before he started sleeping in the bus shelter. She thinks about whether there was a house in the suburbs with a wife and children. Maybe even a dog. It is easy for her to imagine Harry with a dog. She tries to imagine how Harry might feel and then she tries to hear how those feelings would sound as music. When she hears music she tries to separate it into notes.

By the time she gets off the bus she is no longer tired from work and her time spent with Denis. She takes a glass of water and sits at the piano. Beethoven sits beside her. The few other ghosts left make themselves comfortable on the couch.

She starts with scales. Just a few to warm up her hands and get her ear in focus. Then she plays her symphony. Those few notes she has discovered that feel like hers. She takes a page prepared with carefully drawn lines and writes in her notes.

It's slow work. She tries to be neat, but neatness has never been one of her strong points. She tries to remember the passage of notes but finds she can only remember two at a time. Her excitement wears off and she gets tired. Her head starts to swim and her eyes lose focus. She carries on until she can no longer see. Until her eyes are closing of their own accord. Then she goes to bed.

Harry wakes up in his bus shelter. It's morning. He can tell by the sound of the traffic without even opening his eyes. He feels the wood of the seat beneath him, warmer than the concrete of the street. He knows where he is. He knows it's morning. He has no idea how he got to where he is.

His stomach is hard and cold and empty. Harry doesn't care. He lies, still with his eyes closed and thinks in an hour or so he'll get up and check out the bin. There'll be something to eat in the bin and the bin is about as far as Harry's planning to go today.

When Harry opens his eyes the traffic is moving past him and the bus shelter is around him. His mouth is dry and foul. He is thinking about how it will be to stand. He wants to rinse his mouth at the water fountain behind the shelter but then he hears a sound. A familiar tap tap sound that causes him to sit up straight.

It's her but there's no pram. Just her. Harry nearly asks her the time. Opens his mouth, almost gets the words out. And then she's past and walking towards the Junction. She walks a lot faster without the pram. Harry leans his head back against the shelter. He shuts his eyes. It's all wrong her walking past without the pram. All wrong.

When she wakes she tries again. A cup of coffee, a piece of toast and a few more notes. The notes look small but still significant as she writes them on the page. She's so pleased with her progress. It really isn't much. Not even a page. But it feels like hers. Beethoven nods to her. Reassures her. This music she's writing is not copied from anything she's heard. This music is hers. And Harry's.

When Harry dares to look again he sees a man standing nearby, waiting for a bus. His voice is coarse and dry but he gets the words out. "What's the time exactly?" The man jumps a little. Stammers out that it's somewhere around ten. Harry explains he needs to know the time exactly. His voice is getting clearer with use. A bus pulls in and the man gets on, moves away, before Harry has the chance to find out the time exactly.

Perhaps, a year or so ago, Harry would have got on that bus with that man. Would have followed him until the man revealed the time exactly. He would have ignored the shouts from the driver in his pursuit of the exact time. Perhaps he should have got on the bus today. Gone somewhere. Somewhere where his body won't hurt so much.

But Harry doesn't get on the bus. He doesn't do that any more. It didn't really occur to him to try until the bus was moving away. Harry walks towards the Junction. He forgets he planned to stay close to his shelter. Forgets he was going to rinse his mouth and check the bin. On days like today, he decides, it's probably best to stick to the routine.

Harry calls to cars as he walks. "What's the time exactly?" The cars have their windows up against the cold wind. Probably have their heaters on too. Nobody is going to let that cold air into their cars just to tell Harry the exact time. Harry keeps shouting anyway.

On the footpath people walk with their heads down and their arms wrapped around themselves. They walk quickly and don't stop to listen to Harry's question. Don't stop for anything.

Harry walks the length of the mall. He walks back again. No one tells him the time. Not exactly. Someone yells over their shoulder that it's half past ten, another that it's nearly eleven. But nobody does as Harry asks. Not until the woman. The woman who walks to Harry. Who hands him a takeaway cup filled with hot soup. She tells him it's seven minutes past eleven. Harry says thank you. The woman says you're welcome and walks away. Harry sits to drink his soup. He sips slowly and hopes that each sip will stay where it lands.

Harry spends the day sitting in the mall. He sits and waits. Concentrates on the soup in his belly. It's cold and blowy but the soup in Harry's belly is important and he wants to keep it there. So he sits. Closes his eyes now and then. Watches the people hurry past him. Before long the light is fading and Harry begins to think of more food.

Harry thinks of the restaurant down the hill. Not too far. Harry thinks a little warm rice would do him the world of good.

He walks the short distance down the hill and he pushes the heavy restaurant door. There's only one couple sitting at the tables. They pick at the plates in front of them and stare at Harry as he stands at the door.

A man comes from the kitchen to see who has arrived. It's not the man Harry is used to seeing. The man looks at Harry and says, "Yes?" Harry doesn't know what to say. He never used to say anything. They had an unspoken arrangement. Harry would stand by the door and the man would go to the kitchen, come back with whatever he could spare. Harry would nod thank you and leave quickly.

That was how it worked. But this different man doesn't seem to understand how it works. He needs Harry to explain it to him. Harry feels confused. He doesn't have the words to try and explain why he's there so he backs slowly out of the door and goes round the back to wait and see what they throw out at the end of the night.

After work she goes home to the piano to play what she's written. Denis has something on after work and can't meet her. She's not disappointed. She's keen to get back to her symphony. She still likes it when she plays it despite its brevity. She starts to play again with her notes to see if she can settle on any others. She finds a few at the beginning rather than at the end. She takes a new page and starts to write out the notes again. As she copies she makes notes on a separate piece of paper. She writes a few words she thinks might describe Harry, she writes about the weather, about what it must be like to sleep in the cold, so exposed. When she has finished she sits and stares at the keys. She is stuck for what to do next.

Deanne said a few strange things at work today. Statements that made it sound like it was the end of her time there. At first she didn't feel concerned. Now that she has started writing, now that she has Denis' interest and his phone number, the job isn't as important. But now, alone with her piano, she realises that she would miss Deanne. She would miss the routine of going to work. She would miss the money.

She spends her night behind the piano. Mostly just looking at the keys. Beethoven sits with her. The few other ghosts that were left have taken to inhabiting other places, other lives. They're bored with her, with her slow progress. They want to see something new, hear something new. Beethoven is restless too. He's ready to go, but she still needs him, can't let him go. So he stays, quietly sitting, waiting to be released.

He does not talk as they sit together, ghost and girl, but she likes his company. She feels a sense of peace, of good things to come.

Instead of going to bed like she should she decides to visit Harry. She thinks perhaps he may like to hear what she's written. Perhaps she can hum it to him. Or at least tell him of her progress. She does not think about the specifics. Of whether she has the courage to do it.

When she gets to the bus shelter she sees that Harry is sleeping. She stands a little distance from him to watch. He moves a lot in his sleep which is surprising given the narrowness of his bed. He seems to have perfected the art of tossing and turning in limited space.

She squats down on the cold sidewalk and lets her thoughts wander around Harry and what his life might be. Her thoughts move from Harry to her symphony and to Denis. She stays until the chill of the air makes her legs shake and when she leaves for her soft warm bed there is a feeling of guilt, like she doesn't deserve it.

She rises after only four hours of sleep and takes her position at the piano where she stares at what she has achieved and wonders where to go next. There are many ideas but none that stick around. She lets them float in and out until they turn to fears. Fears she will work and work and never finish. Fears she will finish only to discover that she has copied a symphony that belongs to someone else. Fears that she finishes only to be told it's horrible and will never be played.

The day outside looks like a beautiful day. One of those winter days that hold the promise of spring. She decides to take a walk. She wants to see Harry again. Wants to speak to him. She makes two sandwiches with what little she has left in her fridge and heads for the beach.

The day is just as cold but the sun is out. Harry feels the sun is a good thing. He tries not to think about the pain in his body, he tries to think about the sun. He thinks after clock watching he'll go to the beach, lie in the sun. He thinks the sun will take the pain from his body and warm his bones.

People walk a little slower in the sunshine. They listen as Harry asks them, "What's the time exactly?" They lift the arms of their coats to reveal their watches. They stop to pull phones from their pockets. It's too early for clock watching. Not even nine o'clock. Harry asks because he enjoys being answered. Then he sits, waiting for the proper clock watching time.

He feels the sun start to warm the air around him and closes his eyes. He forgets pain and hunger. Perhaps they have gone.

When he opens his eyes the crowd has changed to the ten o'clock crowd, different, slower. When Harry says, "What's the time exactly?" the man with an ear ring through his nose tells Harry it's 10.16 which is enough to get Harry standing and looking through the closest bin while still calling out "What's the time exactly?" There's not much in the bin, half a toasted cheese sandwich, stone cold. Harry takes it at 10.18, walks to the next bin to find a whole bread roll at 10.23.

Harry finishes his cheese toastie at 10.32 and the roll at 10.47. He feels the morning start to melt away. A large cloud blocks the sun and people don't want to stop and tell Harry the time. They walk past, quick as they can, until this one girl. This one girl dressed too cold for the day. Maybe she was feeling hopeful or maybe she just forgot her coat. This one girl shivering and shaking who doesn't really want to stop. Doesn't want to take out her mobile phone but does it anyway. This one girl who tells him it's 11.03. This one girl who is young enough to be his child. Who, if it was his child, Harry would have had to tell, "Put your coat on or you'll catch your death." But Harry doesn't have to say that. Harry says, "Thank you." Then he heads for the beach.

It's busy at the beach. There are a few more than the usual winter surfers in the water and a couple of extra tourists lying on the grass. Mothers push prams up and down the prom like they're late, like they're going somewhere when really they're just going back and forth like the waves. Other people stroll, some hand in hand, some in discussion. Not many are still. It's too cold to be still unless you are well rugged up. Or Harry.

Harry finds himself a spot on the grass that looks warm and dry and isn't too close to anyone else. He watches the gulls and waves. He tries not to think about his body which feels heavy and cold. The ground invites him down and he takes the invitation despite being able to feel the cold coming up through the ground, through his clothes, into his bones. Harry thinks it's a different cold today and that makes it all right to lie down. Yes it's cold but it's not a cold that's trying to kill you.

The sun is warm on his face and this helps him ignore the coolness of the ground beneath him as he drifts off to sleep. He dreams of his mother. She stands over him, watches him lying on the grass. She shakes her head. She looks the same as he remembers her. He thinks she's never changed. All the years he lived with her and all the years he's been away from her, she's never changed.

He says, "Mum, you never change." And she says, "Change? Why would I want to change?" And Harry shakes his head like he knows better because it is the role of the man to have all the answers. He doesn't think about why she should change or if it's all right not to. He just shakes his head. Everyone has to change.

Harry opens his eyes because he can tell she's sitting beside him. He can feel her, smell her. It's not a girl smell, not perfume or anything so obvious. It's something else. Something he can't name or describe but something that tells him it's her.

He does nothing. Tries not to move. He's already opened his eyes so he doesn't want to close them again. He watches the clouds in the sky and wonders if she's brought him anything to eat.

At first she does not see Harry. She has been distracted by the feeling of warm air on her face. By the sun soaking into her clothes. She sits on the wall near the prom and watches the day. She watches people walking past or finding a spot to sit on the grass and that's when she sees Harry and remembers the sandwiches she holds in her hand.

Harry is lying on the grass. It's hard for her to tell whether he's asleep from her position on the wall so she moves to sit next to him. She doesn't want to disturb him so she sits quietly. She tries not to think about the piano. About her desire to get back to it. About her feelings of failure. She tries to just sit and watch and listen.

After a while Harry hauls himself up from his lying position and looks at her. She cannot read his look. Cannot understand if he is pleased or displeased to see her.

Then he starts to cough. He coughs and coughs and coughs. He can't stop. He rolls onto his side, away from the girl, and he spits into the grass. He doesn't look for blood, doesn't want to see. Instead he breathes. Then he wipes his mouth with the back of his hand, sees a trace of blood and quickly wipes his hand on his coat. It's over. He can sit up.

He moves slowly, takes a peek at the girl sitting there near him. The girl looks out at the ocean, not at Harry. She holds a brown paper bag in her lap.

Harry is still hungry. He's got no time for formalities. No time for skirting around the obvious. So he speaks. "What's in the bag?"

The girl jumps. She jerks her head around to Harry. "What?" Harry watches her. She looks at Harry and then at her lap. "Sandwiches." And then, "Cheese." Harry stays silent. "I made them myself."

The two sit a little longer and Harry realises he needs to be a little more blunt so he says, "Well chuck us one here then," and she smiles as she hands him a sandwich.

The sandwich is brown bread. It's cut on the diagonal. Harry looks inside before he bites. It always pays to look inside. There's cheese, pepper, a bit of tomato and a lot of green stuff. Harry looks at the girl. She's eating a sandwich just like the one Harry's holding, only she's taking large bites and chewing quickly. She sees Harry watching and stops chewing. Waits for Harry.

He isn't sure about the pepper. Not sure how his stomach will take it. He's not sure about the tomato either. He's never really liked tomato. Not raw. And then there's all that green stuff. Harry hates green stuff. But she's watching and he's hungry so he takes out what he can and has a bite. Chews carefully. If she is offended she doesn't show it as she starts to eat again.

It's like a school lunch. Harry is sure he could turn his head and see a teacher. Mr Brown perhaps, the science teacher who threw chalk and never liked him. Mr Brown in the playground watching him. Making sure he eats. Waiting for him to do something wrong.

Harry eats slowly to make sure his stomach can take it. He thinks about how he's going to get away from the girl. He doesn't want to move any more furniture. It would be nice to lie back down and sleep but he thinks it will be safer to move away. Maybe back to his shelter or to the library.

Then she starts to speak. "I'm starting to find the notes." Harry has no idea what she's talking about. It makes sense to him that she is a little crazy, the world is full of crazy people, and ones that make sandwiches for homeless men and push pianos down hills are probably a little crazier than most.

The girl says she can hear it in her head all the time now and little by little she's getting it out, getting it down on paper. She talks on and on about it. Harry nods now and then. The girl seems very excited but Harry loses interest in what she's saying. He focuses on the gulls. The gulls have come to see if there are any leftover sandwiches. They crowd in and Harry waits for the girl to shoo them off. She doesn't. Instead she throws them her crusts. Their noise escalates. This stops the girl talking. Or maybe it's Harry's inattention that stops her talking. Harry can't tell, but he's pleased she's stopped.

Harry feels he needs to speak. That somehow he's let her down. He says, "Thanks for the sandwich." The girl stands up, says that she better get going. Harry nods. He should get going too.

The sun is about to disappear behind the buildings and it's time to get off the grass.

It takes a while for the girl to gather her things. He didn't realise she'd brought so much. That it could take so long just to stand and leave.

After she's gone Harry lies back again. Promises himself a moment's rest before he heads back up the hill.

At work she can feel that the end is coming. She has nearly finished her task and Deanne becomes more and more awkward when they chat. Finally Deanne speaks to her. It's almost a relief to have it out in the open. Deanne tells her how sorry she is. How she tried to keep her there. How there's plenty of work but no money. How people don't appreciate librarians. She ends up feeling bad for Deanne. Deanne seems so upset.

Deanne assures her that she can stay until the end of the week. That she can rely on Deanne to give her a good reference. That she was really helpful and great to work with. That she will be missed.

She spends the rest of the week finishing her work. Handing to Deanne anything that she isn't able to finish. She spends an evening or two with Denis. Evenings that become longer and longer but are yet to be the whole night.

She tells herself without a job she will have more time to spend on her symphony. More time to focus on music and Harry. But she knows that after a week or so she will be back looking for another job. That she is now too used to the routine and the money.

Harry is coughing and spluttering and there's someone beside him. Bloody Brian. He's come out of nowhere to be beside Harry. To watch him cough and spit. Harry would have hit him if he had the breath. Bloody Brian should know not to sneak up, not to come from behind. As far as Harry's concerned he could use a good whack.

But instead of Harry hitting Bloody Brian it's Bloody Brian whacking Harry on the back. Trying to help. Always trying to help but not often helping as far as Harry's concerned.

Bloody Brian is pushing a bottle of water into Harry's hands, telling him to take a small sip. Harry tries to push it away, he tries to get to his feet. The world spins. It's black with red angry spots. Then flashes of white. And then quiet.

She does nothing for the first three days. She sleeps, she eats. She stands looking out at the sliver of ocean she can see. Denis rings and asks her how her symphony is going. He tells her he misses seeing her at school. She lies and says it's going well. She makes her unemployment sound like the opportunity she thought it would be. All the time in the world to write and focus on her music, she tells him.

She decides she needs a routine. That it is time to enforce her own structure on the days. She writes it out in half hour blocks and fills in what needs to be done and when. Writing a symphony will become a job. An eight-hour-a-day job. She examines her new schedule with everything she thinks she needs to do neatly allotted and accounted for and she tries to convince herself of the freedom of working from home while in reality she is missing Deanne and the school.

She checks the time and discovers that she should be working so she takes her notes to the piano and sits in front of the keys. She does little and excuses herself because it is the first day and first days at new jobs are always tough. She writes a few notes and plays a few scales. She thinks about Harry and Denis. She even thinks about Mark and resolves to try and continue that contact. A brother is not something to be given up lightly. She picks up her schedule to make a time for phone calls and realises it's time for a break.

It is during her break, as she sits away from the piano, cup of coffee in hand, that she starts to think again about the shape of her symphony. She closes her eyes and there it is. She sees it all. She sees the end. The shape is dancing before her eyes, it's hard for her to put a finger on it, hard for her to see the individual notes but she can definitely see where it is all heading. It's a blur of colour and noise, instruments soaring together in triumph and dying down in desolation and despair. It's so beautiful, there in front of her closed eyes that she thinks she will cry.

She sits at the piano, chipping, chipping away. Searching for the right notes, checking the notes, writing them down, checking again. She loves what she is doing. Loves the sound she is creating. She has abandoned the notion of being neat as she writes out the music. This allows her to write on the sides of the page. She writes phrases that will inform the orchestration. "Like rain," or "feeling pain."

From the outside a stranger would not hear, would not understand, what she is doing. It is a string of notes, rarely are there two together, and the tune is not much of a tune. But in her head she can see where the notes are leading, how they will work in the hands of an orchestra. She can see that what she is writing will become beauty one day and she feels pleased with herself. Beethoven, ever faithful sitting beside her, looks pleased too.

She works for so long her back begins to ache. She starts to take regular breaks, walking away from the piano, stretching her arms above her head. Her day schedule includes a walk along the beach and as difficult as she finds it to leave the warmth of the flat and the promise of the piano, she understands that she needs the air, needs to see something other than the walls of her home.

Beethoven encourages her walks. Encourages her to leave the apartment and leave him in peace for a short while. She doesn't take it personally. She walks along the prom and then up onto the headland. She feels alive and happy. When she gets home she calls Denis.

Denis invites her to a concert at the school. A free concert, played by students. She can think of nothing better than to sit with Denis and listen to music.

It takes a while for Harry to realise he's in hospital. At first all he knows is that it's quiet. And clean. Then he knows it's bright and he no longer feels cold. He doesn't feel warm either but there is no cold. This feels unusual.

There are people. They come and go. Sometimes they try to talk to him but he doesn't want to listen. Doesn't want to talk. Occasionally Harry tries to move. His limbs are heavy and comfortable. They want to rest. So Harry sleeps.

And then he wakes to find he is still in hospital and he doesn't want to be. He looks for his clothes. For anything that might belong to him. There is nothing. Behind the curtain that surrounds his bed Harry can hear coughing, moaning. And then there's Bloody Brian.

Bloody Brian swings back the curtain. He smiles at Harry. Tells him he's looking good. Asks him how he feels. Harry doesn't feel like smiling. He says, "Bloody Brian." Bloody Brian keeps smiling. Asks him if he's hungry. Harry has to nod. It's just occurred to him that he is.

The food Bloody Brian brings looks pretty unappealing but it's warm and there's a lot of it so Harry shovels it in while Bloody Brian talks about how Harry's getting on in years now and needs to start thinking about looking after himself. Harry asks him "What's the time exactly?" Bloody Brian checks the clock on the wall. It's 3.18 p.m. Harry doesn't ask how long he's been there. Bloody Brian will tell him anyway.

It's been three days and Bloody Brian says he'll need to stay two more. He says it's important Harry is really well before he leaves or he'll just get sick again. He tells Harry to relax and enjoy the bed, enjoy the food, maybe have a chat with some of the other men in the room. Harry asks about his stuff. Bloody Brian tells him it's safe and he'll bring it in when it's time for Harry to leave. Then he smiles. He's trapped Harry and he knows it. Harry says, "Piss off, Bloody Brian," and Bloody Brian smiles like he's just been paid a compliment. Then he leaves.

It's strange to be back in the school. Denis has given her directions to part of the school she's never been in before. It feels so completely familiar and then so strange, all at the same time. She starts to feel uncomfortable and unsure of herself. Seeing Denis helps. His smile, his body close to hers. She finds she is able to sit and enjoy the music in the company of Denis.

The music remains nameless to her because it seems that everyone else in the room is familiar with it and she decides not to advertise her ignorance. She understands that she has been focused on symphonies and what she is listening to is not a symphony. She thinks this makes her ignorance acceptable and she tells herself she is relaxed and enjoying it and she doesn't need to tell anyone that she doesn't know what she is listening to. She enjoys the music but more than that she enjoys the feeling of Denis next to her. Denis, so warm and solid, who has been bold enough to reach over and hold her hand.

It's been a long time since someone held her hand like this. She likes it. Likes it a lot.

At the end of the concert she stands with Denis and some of his friends. He still holds her hand. She still likes it. The friends talk about music in terms she does not understand.

Denis wants to take her home. She wants to let him. She takes him past Harry's shelter but Harry is not there. They talk about Harry. Talk about how he manages to sleep there. They take turns to lie on the bench. They kiss sitting next to each other in Harry's space.

At her home they spend a long time on her couch. She doesn't offer to play her symphony to him and he doesn't ask. They talk of themselves. They kiss. Denis remembers he has classes in the morning. She urges him to stay but he is perhaps wiser than her in the art of starting a relationship. He leaves quickly. She lies on the couch, enjoying the warmth he's left behind.

Harry gets through the next two days by eating and sleeping. He doesn't talk to the other men. They don't seem to make much sense and he's not looking for any friends. He tries to clock watch. Calls from his bed, "What's the time exactly?" to anyone that passes by the room, anyone who comes in to poke him or pass him medication. Sometimes they tell him, sometimes they say, "Shhh!" sometimes they just pretend they haven't heard.

Once a day someone comes to shuffle him off to the showers. They wait while he gets clean and dry and dressed then they shuffle him back. Harry begins to miss his bench and the company of cars. He misses people passing by. Ordinary people, dressed in work clothes or jeans. He even begins to miss the cold of the mornings. The chill of the night air.

Bloody Brian returns like he said he would with a bag of Harry's stuff. His clothes have been cleaned and no longer look like Harry's. Bloody Brian tells him he looks well and that he's done real good by staying in the hospital and that it's time they sat down to chat about what to do next. Harry takes his clothes and the bag of his belongings and tells him to piss off. Bloody Brian sighs and goes to wait outside while Harry gets dressed.

It's not easy getting dressed. The clothes feel wrong and Harry is still a little wobbly. He practises moving around the bed so he can walk past Bloody Brian like he's on top of the world. He checks the bag for his CD and his fork and then arranges his belongings in his pockets. He pulls back the curtain and walks out of the room. Walks past Bloody Brian like he hasn't even seen him. Bloody Brian follows, tells him he'll give him a lift.

Anywhere he wants to go. Harry wants to make his own way but Bloody Brian says it looks like rain and suggests he drop Harry at the Junction.

Bloody Brian talks the whole way. Harry tries not to listen. He doesn't want to hear about housing, about moving away from the beach. He gets out of the car as soon as he can and heads straight for his bus stop. He's looking forward to sitting down. To being by himself with the traffic in front of him. He rounds the corner and starts up the hill. And then he sees what they've done.

Harry knows why they did it. He's seen it done before. He's heard all the talk about the Olympics coming. He's seen them cleaning up the buildings and the streets. But still it's hard to take. It's a quiet bus stop. Not many use it. And Harry kept it clean, kept his things in order. He wasn't rude to people who came to sit in there. Didn't hurt anyone. He even tidied up after those school kids who left their chip packets lying around.

But there it is. To others it would look just the same. But to him, it's all been ruined.

The outside of the shelter has not been changed. Only the seat has been altered. They've left that comfortable old wood bench and added arm rests. Curved metal arm rests that divide the seat. The arm rests are painted dark green, the same colour as the wooden bench. Harry knows they did it to him. That they want to get rid of him. How can he lie down on a bench like that?

Harry looks around for his things. His blanket, a few spare clothes. His toothbrush. It's all gone. He can't bear to sit in the changed seat so he sits on the concrete beside it. Bloody Brian. If he hadn't been in the hospital they wouldn't have done it. He could have stopped them. How, he doesn't think about. He just knows if he was there he could have stopped them.

Harry sits on the ground beside the new bench and he says goodbye to his bus shelter. He'd been pretty happy there. In summer he would find a pair of old sunglasses and sleep with them on so the bright sun wouldn't hurt his eyes when he woke up. He watched that baby grow and that woman he liked to pretend was Jules, turn into a mother. He watched the cars and the buses and the people heading to work. That bench was his bed, his couch, his kitchen table. And now it's gone. All of it gone. Just like that.

It becomes clear to her after half an hour of sitting at the piano that today is not a music writing day. She walks to the shops instead, looking into windows and watching couples holding hands with a feeling of pleasure because she is now one of those hand-holding couples. At the local CD shop a poster catches her eye. It advertises a performance at the Opera House of Beethoven's *Eroica*.

She thinks of Beethoven, resting back at her apartment. How pleased he would be to see his work performed. She thinks of Harry. How much he has liked the CD she gave him.

Getting the tickets is easy. She doesn't think about the money, about her dwindling extras fund and the meagre payments she now has to live on. She just gets the tickets. Checks the date. The performance is tomorrow. She is confident she will be able to find Harry, convince Harry, by then.

She makes her way up the hill to Harry's bus stop. It's the middle of the day and she understands that it's unlikely Harry will be there but she thinks she could wait or leave a note. She wonders if Harry can read. She tries to recall the last time she has seen Harry. It was the sandwich day. It does not occur to her that finding Harry will be hard. Much harder than buying those tickets.

She does not notice the changes until she gets right to the bus stop. They must have come that morning because nothing had changed the night before. Harry is not there. Harry's belongings are also not there. And the bench. The old wooden bench has been divided in a way that no one, not even Harry, could sleep on.

She looks to the park behind the bench hoping to find signs of Harry but there is nothing. She stands and does the calculation. She has 27 hours to find him and get him to the concert with her.

One of these hours is spent sitting in his bus stop watching the day grow darker and colder. She walks home via the ocean, searching benches and doorways for Harry.

She does not think to call Denis. The ticket is for Harry. She must find Harry. She spends a little time with her music. She sees the events of the day as fodder for her symphony. These things will inform her music. She understands that. She welcomes it.

She sleeps because she is tired and she doesn't know what else to do.

In the morning she resumes her search for Harry. Beethoven floats behind her. The concert has given him a new burst of energy and interest in her life. She finds Tony at the beach. He hasn't seen Harry for a few days. Tony suggests the Cross.

It's a miserable day. Intermittent rain pounds down and she wishes for an umbrella as she runs from shop awning to shop awning.

She's never liked the Cross, always avoided it. She feels nervous there, unsure of her steps and herself. She prefers the cleanliness of the beach. The open sky, the harmless tourists. In the Cross the tall buildings crowd into her and the people look hard, angry. She quickly walks the main drag and sees no sign of Harry. There are others of course. Many others, men and women, young and old, who have a similar look to Harry, but are not Harry.

She walks home to save the train fare, still unwilling to give up on finding Harry.

At home she showers and changes into dry clothes. The most suitable clothes she can find for the Opera House. Beethoven waits at the door. Anxious she not be late for his concert.

She puts the tickets carefully into her pocket and heads to the bus stop. Her legs are tired from her day and it feels a struggle just to get to the bus, just to stand and wait. She is disappointed that she's been unable to find Harry. That her vision of them both, side by side at the Opera House listening to Beethoven, will not happen. It feels like defeat to take those final two steps onto the bus.

She takes a window seat, still hoping but no longer expecting, to see Harry. And there he is. Sitting at his bus stop. He looks like he's waiting to catch the bus but the bus goes straight past and Harry doesn't move. She reaches for the bell too late and has to run back to Harry from the Junction, Beethoven jogging behind.

She runs because time is running out to get to the concert and she runs because she is worried that by the time she gets there, Harry will be gone.

Harry has been drinking. She smells it as soon as she gets near him. She has no time to think about it. Another bus approaches and she waves it down, telling Harry to come with her.

On the bus Harry tells her he can't go to a concert. She tells him he has to and for reasons neither of them really understands he obeys.

It's a long walk from the bus to the Opera House. She drives him forward, encourages him on with chatter of the music they are about to hear and questions as to whether he's been there before. She doesn't have time to stop, to take in the beauty and comfort of the Quay. She doesn't have time to think about how long it's been since she was last there, how little she's needed it lately.

Beethoven turns circles behind them. He is impressed by the structure of the Opera House, pleased by the number of people walking in to hear his music. He is awed by the Quay and the Bridge. He turns around and around, taking it all in.

Harry stays silent. He keeps his head down, his eyes on his feet. But he keeps moving and she is grateful for that.

People stare of course. They stared on the bus and they stare on the way to the Opera House. They stare as they walk through the doors. They stare as they take their seats. They whisper too. She hears them behind her, around her. She hopes Harry's hearing is worse than hers. That he is saved from these whispers.

The lights go down and the conductor steps up. Everyone claps politely and there is an agonising wait as musicians lift instruments and shift in their chairs. Then a moment of silence. A long, slow moment of silence. She holds her breath as the music starts.

At the first note, Harry lifts his face towards the sound as if it were sunshine. He closes his eyes and the muscles on his face completely relax.

The people around them stop shifting in their chairs, stop their disapproving glances, their quiet but audible complaints. She relaxes into her seat. She observes the conductor, watches the instruments moving in the hands of the musicians. She sees the focus on their faces. She watches them play and feels their joy. The conductor spreads his attention around the orchestra, wildly waves his arms then holds them still.

Harry's eyes flicker open for a moment to take in the musicians in front of him, the Opera House around him, then they close again. She is pleased to know he is not sleeping. She tries to imagine what Harry is feeling and seeing.

Beethoven strains in his seat beside her. He is desperate to join the orchestra, to get close to this music he wrote so long ago. She looks to Harry, sitting with his eyes closed, his face lifted towards the music and she closes her eyes too. With her eyes closed she stops hearing Beethoven's music. Beethoven the ghost is released. Finally allowed to be free. To leave her. He drifts up towards the stage, towards the musicians and the conductor.

She sits with her eyes closed and she feels him leave her. She stops hearing his music and she starts to hear her own.

ACKNOWLEDGEMENTS

I read a number of books during the writing of this one. Used, and quoted, in this text is *The Vintage Guide to Classical Music* (Jan Swafford, 1st ed. 1992 Vintage Books, New York). Other books include *Beethoven's Hair* (Russell Martin), *Beethoven and his Nine Symphonies* (George Grove), *The Beethoven Compendium* (Barry Cooper), *The Symphony* (Robert Simpson) and *Secret Lives of Great Composers* (Elizabeth Lunday).

The characters and events in this book are a work of fiction. However, the Olympics really did come to Sydney, a beautiful old bus stop near Bondi Junction really was modified to discourage anyone sleeping there and homelessness continues to be a very real problem.

My thanks to Chris for being there from the first to last draft of this book and to our three children, Zeke, Henry and Milo who were and continue to be very welcome interruptions to my writing. Thanks also to Deborah and John for your time and comments and to Joe, my walking/writing partner.

Thanks always to my parents for everything they do and to the RRP team for helping to make my work days fun.

Special thanks to Spinifex Press, Renate, Susan and Pauline for your support, input and encouragement.

Other fiction from Spinfex Press

Glory
Sarah Brill

She lies in the bed and she is sick. Sicker than she's ever been. But with the sickness comes a pain and in that pain she finds a glory. And it's the glory that gets her through. When her body heals and she is out of hospital and home with her family, she needs to seek out a new glory, a stronger glory. She finds it in starvation. A story of one girl's struggle with herself, her life and her family. And the story of a family's struggle with a daughter/sister they can never hope to understand.

"Youthful suicide, anorexia and drug abuse are dangerous topics for the novelist to handle … Playwright Sarah Brill boldly and successfully tackles all three in this first novel … A writer to watch."
—Lucy Sussex, *The Age*

"Sarah speaks from the inside of a muddled teenager's head. And which teenager is not muddled? Every parent, however confident must read this book—it will open up their minds and help them understand their children. If you think you know your kid—this book will expose the reality—you really don't."
—Amazon, reader review

ISBN: 9781876756253

Lillian's Eden
Cheryl Adam

In *Lillian's Eden*, debut novelist Cheryl Adam takes the reader to the Australian rural post-war era through the life of a family struggling to survive. With their farm destroyed by fire, Lillian agrees to the demands of her philandering, violent husband to move to the coastal town of Eden to help look after his Aunt Maggie.

Juggling children, two households and her trying husband, Lillian finds an unlikely ally and friend in the feisty, eccentric Aunt Maggie who lives next door.

"This is engaging and tragic-comic historical fiction showing how the lives of women in regional Australia were limited by the laws and social norms of the era. There is a large number of vividly drawn characters, some subtle treatment of the importance of female solidarity in dark times, and a really impressive picture of the dynamics of families, couples and marriage."

The Age/Sydney Morning Herald

"*Lillian's Eden* opens a magic door into 1950s rural Australia. It is an elegantly-paced, colourful excursion down memory lane, complete with money worries, murky family secrets, an eccentric old aunt, an abusive, adulterous husband, and a feisty, courageous wife. Tragedy, comedy, farce, tenderness, triumph—and grit."

—Carmel Bird

ISBN: 9781925581676

Parallax
Robin Morgan

She inspected her knitting. "A yarn imagines itself, you know," she murmured, "from separate strands. Every story is made of strands, too, of worlds that keep unfolding simultaneously along the same yarn. You can spot one at a time or, rarely, a multitude swarming—though no yarner can ever glimpse both the individual tale and the swarm at the same moment. Imagination can conceal while it reveals. Sooner or later, though, everything gets used."

In *Parallax*, Robin Morgan's most radiant prose, spare but sensuous, welcomes you into her dazzling imagination. This is a story about storytelling—a set of shorter tales which, like Russian dolls, nest and fit together to reveal a larger one.

A fable for the future, a prediction about the past, *Parallax* is a luscious story that enfolds you and demands immediate rereading the moment you finish, a story that surprises you and invites you to play with the patterns inside its paradoxes, a story whose characters will accompany you for the rest of your life.

"I read it because I started it and did not want to stop. The more I read, the more I did not want to stop. I loved the mixture of frame and stories … the good-natured tone, the wit, the generosity. This is vintage Morgan."

—Ursula K. Le Guin

ISBN: 9781925581959

Murmurations
Carol Lefevre

For the first time since he'd left the island he thought of the starlings massed at dusk in the winter trees behind the children's home. He remembered the rustle of their wings when they twisted in skeins over the fields, or swelled and contracted high above the cliffs, dark wave after dark wave, lifting and falling in a kind of dance. Sister Lucy had said it was a murmuration. He was still quite young, and he had thought the birds were showing him a sign, that there was something written in their fluid patterns.

Lives merge and diverge; they soar and plunge, or come to rest in impenetrable silence. Erris Cleary's absence haunts the pages of this exquisite novella, a woman who complicates other lives yet confers unexpected blessings. *Fly far, be free*, urges Erris. Who can know why she smashes mirrors? Who can say why she does not heed her own advice?

Among the sudden shifts and swings something hidden must be uncovered, something dark and rotten, even evil, which has masqueraded as normality.

"With beautiful, clear-eyed insight, *Murmurations* charts lives edging towards revelation or despair. The women at the heart of these stories have the poise and mystery of figures in paintings. We're drawn into intimacy with them through the grace of Carol Lefevre's benevolent vision and quietly assured prose."

—Michelle de Kretser

"Beautifully conceived and composed, *Murmurations* presents a series of stories that intriguingly fold into each other. There is not a false note here, not a single word out of place, not one detail that is irrelevant. By the end, the hidden griefs, fears and desires of people who are connected but emotionally estranged are revealed in such subtle, unexpected ways, you will want to re-read it straight away, and then again, and again."

—Debra Adelaide

ISBN: 9781925950803

Dark Matters
Susan Hawthorne

When Desi inherits her aunt Kate's house in Brunswick she begins to read the contents of the boxes in the back room. She discovers a hidden life, one which could not be shared with Kate's family.

Among the papers are records of arrest, imprisonment and torture at the hands of an unknown group who persecute her for her sexuality and activism. Scraps of memoir, family history and poems complete this fragmented story.

Can Desi find Mercedes? The woman Kate has loved so much. Mercedes, who had escaped from Pinochet's Chile. Where is she and can she help unravel Kate's story?

"*Dark Matters* is a transformative tour de force; lyrical as Sappho and revolutionary as Wittig in *Les Guérillères*."
—Roberta Arnold, *Sinister Wisdom*

"This is a book of underworlds and infernos, places of execution, practices of erasure and sites of desire. It documents the practicalities of attempting to break lesbian cultures woman by woman, finger by finger and story by story. Against such violence Hawthorne offers poetry as activism, as remedy, as mode of repair. *Dark Matters* is a meteoroid. When it hits, it will make a different world of you."
—Hayley Singer, *Cordite Poetry Review*

ISBN: 9781925581089

*If you would like to know more about
Spinifex Press, write to us for a free catalogue, visit our
website or email us for further information
on how to subscribe to our monthly newsletter.*

Spinifex Press
PO Box 105
Mission Beach QLD 4852
Australia

www.spinifexpress.com.au
women@spinifexpress.com.au